N.D. Gomes graduated from the University of Stirling with a BA in Media & Journalism Studies, and went on to receive her Master's degree in Education in the US She currently works in a public school system to increase educational opportunities for students with special needs. Prior, N.D. Gomes wrote for the London-based online student political magazine, *deAlign* and stage-managed student plays at the Lee Strasberg Theatre Institute in New York City where she attended for two years. Her first novel, *Dear Charlie*, was published in 2016, followed by *Blackbird* in 2017.

Blackbird

N.D. Gomes

ONE PLACE. MANY STORIES

HarperCollins
PUBLISHERS
Since 1817

This novel is entirely a work of fiction. The names, characters and incidents portrayed in it are the work of the author's imagination. Any resemblance to actual persons, living or dead, events or localities is entirely coincidental.

HQ
An imprint of HarperCollins*Publishers* Ltd
1 London Bridge Street
London SE1 9GF

This paperback edition 2017

1

First published in Great Britain by
HQ, an imprint of HarperCollins*Publishers* Ltd 2017

ISBN: 9780008184889

MIX
Paper from
responsible sources

FSC
www.fsc.org

FSC™ C007454

This book is produced from independently certified FSC paper to ensure responsible forest management.

For more information visit: www.harpercollins.co.uk/green

Printed and bound in Great Britain by
CPI Group (UK) Ltd, Croydon, CR0 4YY

This book is for my sister, Olivia.
Your strength and grace amaze me.

BLACKBIRD Playlist

Syml – 'Where's My Love'

Bon Iver – 'Skinny Love'

Amber Run – 'I Found'

Dermot Kennedy – 'After Rain'

Johnny Cash – 'Hurt'

Kaleo – 'All the Pretty Girls'

Syml – 'Better'

Dermot Kennedy – 'Shelter'

Lily Allen – 'Somewhere Only We Knew'

Belle and Sebastian – 'The Fox in the Snow'

Bon Iver – 'Holocene'

Seafret – 'Oceans'

Sia – 'Bird Set Free'

Prologue: 31.12.2015

Thirty-first of December. The end of 2015. That was the night that five thousand blackbirds dropped dead from the sky just before midnight in Beebe, small-town America. Witnesses recalled a dark blanket descending upon the town just moments before the state of Arkansas was propelled into the year 2016. The blanket turned out to be a sheath of dead feathers and battered bodies.

A local preacher blamed it on us – on the evils of modern society. He said the deaths were symbolic of our sins, and that this was only the beginning of the consequences that would follow. Maybe the sudden unexplained death of a species representing freedom and hope really did indicate an ominous future for us all. My science teacher thinks the birds just flew into a jet engine, or that they died because of fireworks.

The southern states in the US went crazy. Locals stocked up on bottled water, first-aid kits and weapons. Some even fled their homes. News reporters broadcasted hysteria-inducing specials on this apocalyptic warning. It happened right in front of me, on my TV screen. I watched it all unfold from my living room in Orkney, like some late-night television drama. But it wasn't. It was real, and it was scary.

I studied the behaviour of the common blackbird in a Life Science class once. I wrote a paper about the history of the species and how they symbolize hope in some European cultures. Many believe birds are the epitome of freedom. Their ability to spread their wings and migrate to a better place during the darker months is something we all envy. If my sister could fly, she'd fly far away from here, and never come back. But she can't fly. And I'm happy about that.

The great Emily Dickinson once said so eloquently, 'Hope is the thing with feathers.'

31 December 2015.

That was also the last night I saw my sister alive.

I lost everything that night.

And I haven't been the same since. We all haven't.

We used to spend every New Year's Eve together, just the two of us. But then we began to drift slowly apart, the years driving us into adolescence and indifference. For years, we battled our way back to how we used to be, and we were there. We had made it. We were close once again, finding ourselves back where we started, just the two of us. We needed nothing else, no one else. We weren't just sisters. We were best friends.

31 December 2015.

We were supposed to spend this one together. It was special for us. I'd picked a movie, bought popcorn – the kind you microwave in a paper bag until it puffs and expands. She'd gone out to see her friends but she'd planned to be back for ten o'clock.

I waited for her. Until half past, until eleven, and even until midnight. I waited in the living room where I could see and hear the front door. The DVD box sat on the floor by the TV unopened. The bag of popcorn lay beside it.

I waited.

But she never came back.

She still hasn't come back.

My name is Alex. I am fifteen years old, and I don't know where my sister is.

Or if she will ever come back.

All I know is that my sister was last seen sometime before 10 p.m. on New Year's Eve two miles from where I stood, watching footage of the birds falling from the sky on our small TV screen in our small living room in a small house on a small island, too far from reality.

They say you can sense when someone you love is in pain or has died. But I feel nothing. So she can't be hurt or dead, right? Even that night, I didn't feel any different going to bed, and I didn't even worry when Dad said she hadn't come home that night. I assumed she had stayed over at a friend's house. I figured she had lost track of time, but my parents were worried. I told them not to be and that she'd be back later that day. I was wrong. She didn't come back. She still hasn't come home.

After they called the police, it was in the local papers that very evening – 'Local Girl Missing'. She wasn't missing. She had just forgotten to call, or something. Missing sounds like she's dead. Who called the newspaper? How do they know things before we do?

I remember the doorbell ringing, and walking slowly to answer it. I remember turning the knob and pulling the door open, expecting to see my sister's smiling face. But it wasn't her. It was two policemen. One was older, scruffy-looking. He was the one that was clutching a small spiral-bound notepad in his hands. But it was the younger one who took my parents' statement.

I watched as my mother put her hand over her mouth to stifle her sobs as she and my dad spoke softly to them. They told the officers that my sister had gone to a party with her friends and not come home. They told them they were worried about her. They told them they were scared. They hadn't told me that. They had told me that there was nothing to worry about, that she'd come home. But now they're lying. Or did they lie to me?

I remember that the older policeman wasn't looking at them. He was watching me. And he had this look on his face that I couldn't figure out – pity? Sadness? Indifference?

Either way, I will never forget his face. Or my mother's when they told her that she needed to wait twenty-four hours before it can become an official missing persons case. Both will haunt me forever. I felt confused at first, like I had heard him wrong. 'Missing persons case.'

I thought it was my sister playing jokes as she usually did. But then I saw the policeman's face, and I knew it was true. Then I felt like all of the air had been violently sucked out of my body and I couldn't breathe. It's a strange feeling when someone tells you the person you love most in the world has vanished. It's like you've been stripped from your body, and you're floating above watching everything happen. Because you never think it will happen to you – that it *is* happening to you.

Being Orcadian, you are somewhat sheltered from that world. The world where evil is normal. Our island is small. Too small. Everyone knows everyone. But that is what's so hard to understand. Someone must know where she is. Someone must know something.

She's just staying over at a friend's. That's it. She'll be back tomorrow.

Right?

What if she's not back tomorrow? Or the next day? What then?

These police officers don't know her. They don't know anything about her so how are they going to find her?

I know her. She's my sister. I know her.

She just turned eighteen years old on her last birthday.

Her name is Olivia.

She's finishing school this year and is going to move to London. She's looking forward to beginning her life. She wants to be a dancer with the Royal Ballet Company in London. And she will be, everyone says she dances beautifully. I love to watch her perform. She's mesmerizing. She looks so free – like a blackbird.

Olivia.

Where are you?

Chapter One:

02.01.2016 (morning)

'What time did you last see your sister on the night of the thirty-first?'

The room is cold, dimly lit, in the police station in Stenness near the Barnhouse Settlement. I pull my sleeves down over my hands and tuck them between my legs. How long have I been here? Is it still morning? Why am I here? I don't know anything. I can't share anything. I'm as in the dark as them.

I can feel my eyelids twitching, but I can't stop it. I try opening them a little wider.

'Alexandra?'

'Alex.'

'Alex, what time did you last see your sister on the night of the thirty-first?' The police officer shifts in his seat like he's uncomfortable, but his eyes never leave my face. Maybe he's the reason my eyes are twitching. I remember him from yesterday. I remember the expression on his face.

'Detective Birkens, is it?' I cautiously ask.

'Detective Inspector Birkens. I'll be leading the investigation into your sister's whereabouts. We met yesterday, very briefly.'

'I remember.'

'Sorry I had to get you up so early today.'

My body weighs heavily in the chair beneath me. My eyelids are starting to drop. It really is cold in here. There's a breeze coming in from somewhere. The detective doesn't seem to notice. What is the difference between a policeman and a detective anyway? Should I ask him?

'Are you OK? Do you want anything to drink – water, tea, a Coke?'

No, I just want to go home.

The door clicks open and the younger policeman from yesterday steps into the room. He closes the door behind him, and leans against the wall by the door-frame. Now he's watching me too. Everyone is.

'Where are my mum and dad?' I eventually ask.

'They're in the next room. They're talking to another police officer.'

'Why are we here?'

'Because it's been over twenty-four hours since Olivia was initially reported missing, so it's now treated as a missing persons case.'

'Case?'

'It's just a formality,' smiles the younger policeman.

The detective inspector turns to him then looks back at me. 'So back to Hogmanay evening,' he says.

'We ate dinner together.'

'What time was this?'

'Around half past five–'

'Who's we?'

'Me, Olivia, Mum and Dad.'

This chair is really uncomfortable. I arch my back for some relief then try to settle back into the frame. There needs to be a cushion or something on the base.

I want to go home.

'How would you describe the atmosphere at dinner?' he says, looking up from his notepad.

'What do you mean?'

'Was there tension?'

'Tension between who?'

'Between her and your father, or between her and your mother . . . or between you and her?'

'We didn't fight, if that's what you mean.'

'And your parents?'

'No, nothing like that. Dinner was normal. We ate at the dining table, talked about normal stuff – work, school, friends, then she went upstairs to shower and get dressed; while Mum and I washed up and dried the dishes.'

We always ate together on Hogmanay evening, even if everyone had plans. We sat down together for one last time before the old year ended and a new one began. That time was special to us. This year, Olivia helped cook a roast with my dad. She chopped the potatoes and carrots, while my dad made a glaze and tied the meat together with twine. I don't know why he did that. But it tasted good in the end.

My sister and my dad are really close. They enjoyed cooking together, while I preferred to set the table. They go for walks together while I stayed home.

They watched movies on the sofa together, while I read in my bedroom. My dad was devastated when Olivia told him she was moving to London, like he was losing his best friend. I was still going to be here. But that didn't seem to be enough for him.

'And where was your father during this?'

'He was upstairs in the bedroom or his work study, I think.'

'Did your parents go out on Hogmanay?'

'They went to the Legion for their annual dinner and dance. They go every year.'

'What time did they leave the house?'

'After Olivia left. Maybe around quarter to seven?'

'Olivia went straight to Emily Morrison's house?'

'That's what she said she was going to do.' My throat feels warm, the words hot in my mouth. Does he know I'm lying?

He looks at me for a moment too long, like he knows.

'And your parents?'

'Yes?'

'When did you see them next?'

'At home, the next morning.'

'And you?'

'I was at home. Olivia and I were supposed to watch

a movie together around ten . . . after she got back from Emily's. We were going to ring in the New Year together this year. I'd bought –'

'Ten, you said?'

'– Popcorn.'

'What?'

'Nothing, never mind. Yes, ten.'

He scribbles in his notepad then looks up at me again.

'Did you see the headline about the blackbirds?' I ask, feeling my palms start to sweat.

'No.' He clears his throat and slides the notebook on the table in front of him. 'And what did you do at home before ten?'

'Before?' Oh no. 'I told you, I just stayed in,' I say, fidgeting with the bottom of my shirt. I loop the fabric around my finger, feel it stretch beyond its limits.

'Alone?'

Why is he asking me all these questions?

'Yes, alone.'

'Alex.'

'What?'

'You wouldn't be the only fifteen-year-old who drank alcohol on Hogmanay with their friends while their parents were out the house.'

'I didn't do that.' I shrug, glancing up at the door. Is he sure they can't hear us?

He leans back in his chair and crosses his leg over his knee. He's waiting for me to say something, waiting for me to confess all my sins. 'I'm not going to arrest you for lying to your parents.'

'OK fine, I wasn't alone all night. Andy and Siobhan came by.'

'What time?'

'After everyone had left, so around seven.'

'And what did you do?'

'We watched telly until around half-past nine or quarter to ten.'

He doesn't believe me. He knows I'm lying. I'm going to get in trouble and be grounded for the next ten years of my life.

'I'm not here to arrest you for underage drinking. I'm just trying to get an idea of where everyone is when Olivia goes missing. Whatever you say won't get back to your mum and dad. Understand?'

I nod, and relax my shoulders. 'Exactly what you said – we drank alcohol while my parents were out of the house.'

'Who brought the alcohol?'

'Nobody. My dad has a stash of beers in the garage. He wouldn't notice any were missing, and if he did he would never ask me because then he would know that I know that he drinks beer in the garage when Mum isn't looking.'

'She doesn't like him drinking?'

'She put him on a diet earlier this year. He has diabetes.'

He nods, and writes something down on his notepad.

I lean my body a little to the left to try and see what he's writing but then he scoops up the cover and places it over the pad.

'And how many beers did you have?'

'Just one –'

He raises his eyebrows and looks at me, waiting.

'OK, more than that. Maybe three.'

'Last question.'

Thank god. 'OK.'

'If your sister was upset about something – and I'm not saying she is – where would she go?'

'You mean, like a secret hiding place? You think she's hiding somewhere?'

'Maybe.'

'She wouldn't do that. She wouldn't want to scare us like that.'

'Even if she was upset, maybe even scared?'

Why would my sister be scared? Was she in trouble and she never told me? Who's scaring her?

'Her boyfriend's house –'

'James MacIntosh, right?'

'Yes. Her friend Emily's, the dance studio where she takes classes – they have an open studio in the afternoons when anyone can go – the library, the Ring –'

'– of Brodgar?' asks the younger policeman.

'She likes that, especially around sunrise, before the tourists come, of course,' I smile.

'Of course,' he says.

Birkens is writing in his pad again. His hand must be sore from all the writing. 'Sunrise? That's early.'

'She always wakes up earlier. She doesn't like to sleep late. Not like me. I can sleep all day. Olivia likes to go for a walk in the mornings.'

'Where?'

'Down to the Ring, along the loch, through the woods by Binscarth Farm – there's a little trail there. My dad sometimes goes with her, you should ask him.'

'I'll do that.' He rises from the chair, pushing it back gently on the wooden floor. 'Thank you, Alex. Your mum and dad are waiting outside.'

As he starts towards the door, I call after him. 'Will Olivia be in trouble when she comes home?'

He doesn't turn for a while, just looks straight ahead towards the other policeman or maybe beyond him. Slowly he turns to face me and has a forced smile on his face. 'No, she won't be in any trouble.' He gestures towards the closed door.

When I leave the conference room, Mum and Dad are waiting for me in the lobby of the station. They both stand up when I come out.

'Everything OK?' Mum asks, as she gently tucks a strand of hair behind my ear. She hates seeing me with my hair across my face. She likes it up off my face, in a bun or a French braid like Olivia's.

'What did they ask you?' says Dad, as he digs his car keys out from his jeans pocket.

'Just about Hogmanay night.'

'Well, let's get home,' my mum says, as she wraps her arm around me and nudges me towards the exit.

Walking over, I grab the knob but don't turn it. I have to ask them something, and I have to see their faces when I ask it. 'She's just staying at a friend's, right? We'll find her?'

My mum nods but my dad doesn't say anything. He's not looking at me so I wait for him to say the words.

'Yeah, sure. We'll find her,' he eventually says.

When we reach the house, my dad drops us at the front door. He tells us to go inside and lock the door. He's going to get some posters printed with my sister's face on them.

She's going to be so embarrassed when she comes back.

Scooping up the phone directory, my mum disappears into the living room to start calling people. I think she's called everyone by now.

No one's seen Olivia.

No one knows where she is.

The house seems bigger to me now for some reason. And colder. A shiver shoots up my spine, and I hug myself to keep warm. I shuffle over to the wood burner and load some logs into the furnace. Lighter in hand, I search around for some newspaper to scrunch up. Sliding a paper out from under the TV remote, I kneel back down in front of the furnace and begin ripping pages off. I make only three paper strips to burn with the logs when something catches my eye. Lifting the paper up to my eyes, my sister's name stares back at me. There she is.

Underneath her name is one word, in bold capitals: MISSING. That's all she is now. Missing. She's the missing girl from the Orkneys. The missing persons case that's rocked this small community. That's what the paper is saying.

Olivia.

Where are you?

Come home before this gets any worse.

Chapter Two:

02.01.2016 (afternoon)

I don't push the doorbell, but slam my hand on James's door, needing to feel pain. He doesn't answer. My palm throbbing a little more than I had hoped for, this time I ring the bell. He answers almost immediately as if he'd been waiting for me right behind the door.

He opens his mouth to say something but I get there first. 'Is she here?' I ask, glancing over his shoulder. The TV flickers behind him, crackling against the wall in the hallway.

'Alex, she's not here. I haven't seen her.'

'Are you lying? Are you trying to cover for her? If you are that's fine, just tell her to come home.'

He steps out from the doorway and rests against the edge of the frame. Dark circles have formed around his eyes and his skin is a little paler than usual. 'Look, I really don't think it's anything to worry about.'

'Are you kidding? She's going to be in so much trouble. The police are involved now.'

'I know. They just came to see me.' He pushes his

hands into his jeans pockets and looks out past me, towards the street or the ocean beyond me.

'And?'

'And I told them the same thing. She's not here.'

A large sigh escapes my lungs and I tuck my chin to my chest a little. I had been hoping that she was here, hoping that James would know where she was so we could end all of this. But he knows as little as me. 'Well, when was the last time you saw her? At the party?'

'What party?' He shrugs.

'Euan's party.'

'How do you know about that?'

'She tells me everything. I know she wasn't watching a movie at Emily's house. She went to a party at Euan's house over by Binscarth Farm.'

He digs his hands in deeper into his pockets and smiles slightly, the corners twisting up but not in a way that I find familiar or comforting. 'She tells you everything, does she?'

'Yes . . . I think so.'

'Well, did she tell you we broke up?'

'What?'

'I guess she doesn't tell you everything.'

'This isn't a joke. This is a waste of police time. She could be charged or something, I don't know.'

'I'm telling you the truth. We broke up. I wasn't at that party because I knew she was going. I did my own thing, hung out with the boys from the football club.'

'Why did you break up?'

He frowns, tiny lines forming across his forehead.

I can't imagine them not together. They're all I remember. The two of them and Emily have been friends for so much of her – and my – life. Was this because of London? Had they argued about her moving there? Had he refused to go, or asked her to stay?

'You'll have to ask her. I would like to know myself.'

He looks uncomfortable, his fingers fidgeting in his pockets. I don't know what else to say to him. I came here looking for Olivia, but all I've done is remind him of a time he seems to want to forget.

'Um, well if you do know where she is, please get this message to her. She needs to come home. I doubt she'll be in much trouble now. If she waits too long, she might be.'

'Like I said, I don't know where she is.' He steps back and slowly closes the front door, leaving me all alone on the step.

I turn around and walk down the driveway, glancing back at the house to see if there is any movement behind the curtains. She would have come out if she was there and heard my voice. She'd know everyone was worried about her.

I don't think she's here.

I gaze down the street and wonder if she walked here recently. Why would they break up? And why would she not tell me about it? I'm her sister. We tell each other everything, or at least I thought we were supposed to.

Maybe she told her best friend instead. I need to talk

to Emily. She'd know where Olivia was. She has to; someone has to.

I lightly jog down to the bus stop at the bottom of the road, and check the timetable. My dad's face enters my mind and I can't stop thinking about the look on it when he told me we'd find Olivia soon. He looked like he didn't believe his own words.

The ache comes back, it's dull at first then starts getting stronger. My hand grips the metal edge of the bus shelter as I try to steady myself.

We'll find her.

We'll find her.

The bus pulls up loudly behind me and screeches to a halt. I close my eyes tight, and take a slow deep breath.

One foot at a time. That's all I have to focus on.

The doors swing open. 'Oi, are you getting on or what? I don't have all day.'

My fingers loosen their grip on the shelter side and I push off slightly to turn around. 'Yeah, sorry.'

Fumbling around for change in my coat pocket, I briefly glance up to meet the driver's eyes. He startles for a moment then straightens up his back slightly. 'So sorry, I . . . I didn't see who you were. I'm really sorry for your family's loss.'

'My sister's not dead,' I say, my tone sharper than I'd intended. But she's *not* dead. She's missing, so please don't call it a loss. We haven't lost her. We just can't find her right now.

'Right, sorry. Where are you off to?'

'I need to get to Kirbister Road.'

'I actually don't stop there, this is a number eight. I only go to Guardhouse Park . . . but I'm almost at the end of my shift, and the bus is empty. I'll take you.'

'Thank you,' I say quietly, pulling out silver fifty-pence pieces from my pocket.

'Don't worry about the fare this time.'

I shuffle to the middle of the bus, and collapse down into a navy cushioned seat. My fingers grip the yellow standing bar, again to steady myself.

The loch is on my right, as we head north up the A965. When I look up front, I see the driver's eyes in the rear mirror. But he's not looking at the cars behind us, because there aren't any. He's looking at me. He must recognize me from the local newspapers. We're all in there, the whole family. Our faces and names splashed all over the front, for the whole world to speculate. How did they act so fast? What do they want from us?

Shivering, I turn my body a little towards the window and gaze out. If she's not at Emily's, I don't know where to go after that, what to do. We're in the newspapers, we're on the news – if she's out there, she would see how this is getting out of hand.

Olivia, where are you?

Please come home.

What if she can't come home? What if she's trapped? Is she being held against her will? Do we know the person who has my sister? Were they in their house right now, watching TV or taking a walk on the beach with their dog? Who is the monster? Whoever it is took my sister from me. Took her from the world, when she had so much to give back.

No, no. She's out there. I know she is, I feel it. Or do I?

The bus jolts and I know we're here. The side door pops open, and I'm relieved because I don't have to talk to the driver again, and face his sympathies, his pity.

'Thank you,' I call back as I step off and my feet land on the icy road beneath. I start pounding the pavement up the street and slow down. That's my dad's car. It's parked in Emily's driveway. He's here too.

When I pull in closer, I see Emily at the front door talking to him. I can't hear what they're saying, but she looks a little scared, or maybe nervous.

'Dad!'

He turns around, but doesn't look surprised. 'I told you to stay in the house.'

'You didn't tell me you were coming here.'

'You didn't either.'

'I stopped by James's too.'

'James?' asks Emily.

'Yeah, me too,' my dad mumbles.

I look at Emily, desperate. 'Well, is she here?'

My dad shakes his head.

'I was telling your dad, I haven't seen Olivia since the party on New Year's Eve. Sorry. I would tell you if she was here. It's all over the newspapers, I wouldn't lie about that.'

'Did you know she was going to a party on Hogmanay?' my dad asks me.

I don't want to lie to him, but I don't want him to think Olivia lied to him either. So I ignore his question and turn back to Emily. 'But surely you must know where she could be if she's not with you?' I ask, taking another step towards her.

'Honestly, lately I never know where she is. We haven't been hanging out as much as we used to. So you're asking the wrong person.'

'Who should we be asking?' my father says, his jaw tensing slightly.

'Not me.' She starts to close the door on us, but then stops. 'Sorry, I wish I knew more, but I just don't.'

When the door clicks shut, I turn to my dad. His chin is down at his chest. I know how he feels. Another dead end.

'Dad, we'll find her. She'll come home.'

He nods his head gently, then walks back to his car. I slide in the passenger side and hear a crumpling beneath me. I'm sitting on papers. When I pull them out from underneath I'm faced with Olivia again. It's a photo of her from her birthday dinner in Aberdeen two years ago. We had gone there for the weekend, stayed on Union Street. During the daytime, we shopped, walked along the River Don to watch the occasional salmon spring to the surface, and even visited Dunnottar Castle. It was mesmerizing. The long winding path down to the castle, the cliff drops on all sides.

In the evening, we had eaten early because Dad likes his meals around half four or five, and walked around the city which really seemed to come to life at night. It was too much for me. Too many bright lights, too many big buildings, too many sounds. But Olivia loved it. I thought it too loud, but for her it wasn't loud enough. That's when she decided she wanted to move to London.

Sometimes we could be so different.

'Alex?'

'Sorry, Dad. I was a million miles away. Did you say something?'

'I want to get the flyers up before it gets dark. Will you help me?'

'Of course.'

We start at the academy, taping posters around the entrance beneath the sky-blue sign, under the letters of STROMNESS ACADEMY, on classroom windows, on lampposts on the streets that spill out. Then we drive to the beach, and attach posters to the sides of bins, on car windscreens. We get to the golf club, the tourist office for the Ring of Brodgar and Skara Brae, bus shelters, the ferry docks, and even a couple of hotels. But when we drive to Kirkwall, we have to split up to cover more ground.

My dad takes his time in the pubs, asking revellers if they've seen anyone that looks like Olivia; while I stop by the cafés, The Shore Hotel, Helgis', the iCentre, St Ola Community Centre, even the library. We meet back at the ferry docks, a small stack of flyers still gripped tight in our hands.

It's not enough.

It'll never be enough.

By this time, the sun has almost set. Some lingering strips of amber and blush hover on the surface of the water.

We leave the remaining flyers on a bench outside Julia's Café where Olivia and I got hot chocolate and watched the tourists march down off the boats and head straight for the warmth of Stromness Inn. It's always colder here than people imagine. The climate isn't for everyone. But for those who manage, it's home.

My hands are red raw from the cold. I eventually had to take my gloves off because the tape kept sticking to the fluff, and I was afraid that the flyers wouldn't stick right and fall off.

My dad has several small scratches on his hands which look like paper cuts.

We've been at this for hours now. But why do we feel like we've not accomplished anything at all?

We get home to find the house in darkness and my mum sleeping on the sofa with the phone cradled in her arms. She doesn't look like she's moved much since I left her.

Why is this happening to us?

She stirs and slowly opens her eyes. They're brown and shaped like almonds, like Olivia's. Like mine.

'You're back. Did you put the posters up?'

'Yeah, we did.'

'Did anyone call?' asks my dad, removing the phone from her grasp. He collapses into his armchair and lays the phone down in his lap, gently securing it with his fingers, as if it might fall and break.

'Journalists,' she mutters.

'How did they bloody get our number?' snaps my dad.

'It's a small island, Peter,' she says.

Mum even sounds like Olivia. I think that's where she got her sense of adventure from. They'd gawk at photos in travel magazines together, and linger on Thomson Holidays adverts. I wouldn't be surprised if Mum encouraged Olivia to move to London mainly so she'd have the chance to visit her there. But for my dad, the weekend in Aberdeen was enough. He got his taste of adventure and culture, and he wanted back on the island as soon as possible.

We couldn't afford to fly, so we'd gone on the NorthLink ferry from Kirkwall. It had taken several hours, which was torture for my dad. I remember standing outside, letting the wind battle my hair wildly, and lift the fabric of my shirt. For me, I'd never felt more free in my life. To be surrounded by water on all sides, the sheer magnitude of it, the infiniteness. But for Olivia, it felt like a prison. She always felt trapped by the water because for her, she was stuck on an island.

The phone rings and we all jump, each of us lost in

our own memories of Olivia. My dad grabs the phone and roughly pushes it to his ear, 'Hello? Hello? Olivia?'

His face drops and he slowly hands the phone to me. 'It's Siobhan. Again.'

'Tell her I'm not –'

'Just talk to her, love,' says my mum, taking the phone from my dad and placing it in my hand.

I get up and walk to my bedroom, feeling the carpet soft under my feet. 'Hello?'

'Hey, it's me. Any news?'

'No, it's still the same. No word from her.'

There's a cold silence between us, and I wonder whether she's still there.

I don't know why, but I haven't wanted to talk to her since Olivia went missing. Our conversations, our general interactions just seem so trivial now compared to what me and my family are going through.

Siobhan and I hang out, we talk about boys, we listen to music, we watch her brother's scary zombie films. Sometimes we pick up the other phone in her house and listen to his conversations with his girlfriend.

We don't do *this*.

'Do you feel like coming over tonight? I can invite Andy if you want, that'll cheer you up –'

'I can't tonight. We have a lot going on here. We're waiting by the phone. We're back out tomorrow, early. We're going to go with the police on their search party.'

'Oh . . . do you want me to come?'

'Don't worry about it. I'll speak to you later.' I hang up before she responds.

Is this what happened to Olivia and Emily? Are Siobhan and I growing up, and growing apart?

Am I losing someone else in my life?

Or am I pushing her away?

Chapter Three: 03.01.2016

I wake at quarter past four in the morning. The darkness in my room is cold, and covers me like a thick and heavy blanket, suffocating me. I can't breathe.

Olivia.

I push the covers off, the cool air stretching across my body, but I still feel hot. My feet touch the carpeted floor beneath my bed and I stagger to the window by my dresser. Unlocking the latch, I heave it up above my head. Ice cold air hits my face and I open my mouth gasping for more. Panting, I lean against the window frame and rub the sleep out of my eyes.

Stars still shine bright in the sky above me, and a blinking light slowly moves across the dark canvas. A helicopter probably. Helicopters are common here, bringing oil-rig workers to and from the mainland. My dad works as an aviation engineer for Novotel Helicopters and knew the route well. He'll be gone for weeks, working offshore, then back as if he'll never left. His shifts are long, but he'll always try to be there for birthdays, Christmases, even Parents' Evenings.

He'll be home this week though. He won't go in.

He'll want to be here when Olivia comes home. She *is* coming home.

Suddenly I'm freezing. The cold air becomes too icy, too dark, too suffocating. I grab the edge of the window and pull down, but it sticks. I squeeze tight with my fingers and pull harder. My fingers slip and I wince as I feel my thumbnail bend back. I start clawing at the window, screaming, warm tears stabbing my eyes. It won't close. Why am I crying?

I can't breathe.

Olivia.

Where are you?

My door bursts open and my dad is standing in the doorway. The hallway light shines from behind him, and it hurts my eyes. I shield them with my hand.

I feel his hands around my bare shoulders. 'Alex, are you OK? What's going on?'

I'm still crying.

'I don't know . . . I can't . . . I can't close my window. I'm so cold!'

He reaches up and easily slides it down to meet the ledge. Suddenly it's so quiet. I feel stupid.

I wipe the tears from my eyes, and blink them open. I've already adjusted to the light. 'I'm sorry. I don't know why I over-reacted.'

He kneels down and sits beside me, both of our backs against the window ledge. I put my hands in my lap and interweave my fingers. I'm wearing blue pyjama bottoms with white polka dots, and a pale pink vest.

We sit for a while in silence, neither of us saying a word. Finally, I look up to meet his eyes. He's staring straight ahead at the wall beside my bed. 'Has she called?' I ask him quietly, afraid of his answer.

He shakes his head.

'Dad?'

He doesn't say anything.

'Dad?'

'Yeah?'

'I want to go looking for her today. I want to join the search team.' I wait for him to say no, to tell me I'm too young, too inexperienced for this kind of situation. If this is what it is. But he doesn't.

'OK.'

He gets up and walks out of my room, closing the door halfway behind him. Darkness seeps in again, but I don't care. I don't mind the darkness now. Because I know in only a few hours it will be gone, stamped out by the first rays of sunrise.

We'll find her today.

We need to.

By the time I've showered and changed, it's almost six. I hurry down the stairs and find my dad dressed with his shoes on already. His thick winter coat sits on the kitchen counter next to mine.

'Do you want breakfast before we go?'

I shake my head. He doesn't argue. He hands me my coat and slides into his. We walk past the stairs and he glances up.

'Is Mum coming?'

'No, she's going to wait here in case . . . she calls.' He doesn't sound convinced that she will.

'She will call, right?' I ask.

He doesn't meet my eyes. 'Yes. She'll call.'

I almost ask him to promise, but I don't.

We lock the house, leaving a spare key under the fake pot plant where Olivia knows to look, in case she's lost her key, and get into the car.

There are no other cars on the road. No headlights, no more blinking lights in the sky either. No one else is outside except us.

'Did you sleep at all?' my dad asks.

'A little. You?'

'Yeah, a little.'

I know he's lying.

'Where are we going?'

'The police are searching the woods out by the Binscarth Farm. It's about a mile from the house where the Hogmanay party was. They said we could join them.'

I shiver, feeling the cold draught in from outside. I turn the heat on and open the vent beside me. Lukewarm air flows out and chills me more.

'Will you be warm enough? We'll be outside for a while.'

I tighten the scarf around my neck and tuck my chin down to feel the warm material on my face. 'Yeah, I'll be fine.'

'We can go back if you want? Maybe you can join later in the morning or –'

'No, I'll be fine.'

I feel guilty. I shouldn't feel cold. I shouldn't want to go back to my warm bed. My sister is out there somewhere, probably freezing and all alone, maybe even injured. I pinch my hand, pressing down hard until I feel a little pain. That's what I deserve.

We take a right onto a dirt road and feel the tyres struggle on the icy stones. My dad shifts into a low gear and eventually we reach the top. Bright lights and crowds of people fill our windscreen. Hats, scarves, gloves, walking boots, torches, walking sticks. Everybody came out today, all in search of my sister.

'Wow,' mutters my dad as he edges through the crowd to find a parking spot.

'Right there,' I say, pointing to a clearing under the trees.

We swing in and quickly shut off the engine. Warm air stops blowing and the cold immediately closes in again.

Opening the door, people start coming towards us. They must have recognized our car because they're all standing around us, telling us they're sorry.

Sorry for what?

Sorry for our loss? Have we lost Olivia? We're all here to find her, so why are people sorry? Perhaps they know deep down inside that what we find may not be what we're ready for.

I wait for my dad to say something, but when I look over I see his lips trembling. He opens his mouth, looking like he might finally speak, but then he closes it again and just nods.

I walk over to him and take his arm. Together we walk through, the crowd parting as we pass. Hands touch my shoulder, squeeze my arm, words of sympathy fill the air around me like the cold chill pressing in.

'Thank you for coming,' I say quietly, occasionally exchanging eye contact with people.

I recognize them all. My headmistress, the old man with the dog who owns the newspaper shop on Main Street, the attractive blonde woman from the tourist office, my dad's work colleagues, my mum's friends and their husbands, Mr Sheffield my sister's music teacher, the redhead who owns the dance studio where my sister used to go. They're all here. They're here with us, for us.

Siobhan is in the back, waving at me. She wants me to stand with her. But I don't move. I'm not here to be social. I'm here for one purpose only – to find my sister. Siobhan is still waving, so I turn and walk away.

We see DI Birkens and his partner, a younger officer.

'You didn't have to come out today, Mr McCarthey. We would have kept you updated,' says Birkens.

'She's my daughter' is all my dad says in response.

Birkens nods in agreement and starts walking back towards his car. His partner follows us. He reaches out his hand to shake my dad's. 'We met before, but you might not remember me. I'm Dave Allans. I'm assigned to this case too. Don't worry, we're going to do everything we can to find your daughter alive –'

'Alive?' I repeat. Was that even a question? She *has* to be found alive.

'Well, after forty-eight hours, the chances are significantly –'

Birkens coughs loudly, then looks at Allans who stuffs his hands in his coat pockets and looks down at the ground. As we walk over to the bonnet of the car, Allans gently touches my shoulder. 'It'll all be OK.'

Birkens pulls out a faded map and rests it against the bonnet, pointing to a large dotted area on the map. 'Here is Stan McGregor's farm and here's Binscarth Farm, combined they stretch out four hundred acres, towards The Ring. If she left the Hogmanay party and headed west then she would have had to pass through here. I say we split up into groups and search everywhere. If she's here in this area, we will find her.'

We listen to Birkens as he instructs us to divide into groups of eight to ten and search row by row, in line. I stand next to my dad, his two friends, Mr Sheffield, the postman and his son Jack, and Officer Allans. I hear a whistle blow and then we start moving, as eight at first, fumbling through the woods always a step in front or behind, then finally as one. We hold our torches low to the ground and skim the light over the ground as we walk. Back and forth, back and forth. Our light touches everything, and nothing.

We call my sister's name, round trees and duck under

bridges with enthusiasm, but we find nothing. Soon the sun rises, the red glow spreading through the grass and trees like a blazing fire. We turn off our torches and pull the hoods and hats back away from our eyes. The air is cold, but the sun soon burns bright.

I feel the chilled blades of grass break under my boots and hear the crunch. The breeze pinches my cheeks and flows through my hair. I can hear birds in the distance to my left and when I turn to hear the sweet music, I see a tall birch tree. Then I realize I'm a step or two behind everyone else but I don't hurry to catch up. Instead I stop and stand for a while in front of the big birch.

It's only for a moment at first, but then it becomes clear – the long dark hair, long lean limbs, her graceful gait that reveals her love of dance. She's walking away from me, her hair swaying in the breeze against her back. But then she turns to look at me. The greenish-brown eyes with the amber fleck and the birthmark on her left pupil, the familiar nose that I see in the mirror every day, the pale olive skin and flushed cheeks. She's wearing fitted dark distressed jeans, dark green wellies, and a slightly oversized khaki coat. A navy and cream scarf drapes around her long elegant neck and hangs loosely around her shoulders. She's beautiful.

While her hair curled naturally and subtly around the ends, mine hung straight like a pencil; while her face was a creamy mix of olive hues and rose, mine was pale, freckled and bothered by the odd teen breakout. She was effortless in her style, whereas I studied her magazines and borrowed her clothes. I always felt inadequate next to her, always a step behind like I am today.

Anyone who knew her, or even saw her, would know that she wasn't meant for a place like this. She was meant for something bigger, like Edinburgh or London. We were just lucky to have her for as long as we could.

Me, on the other hand, I would stay here. I would finish school, get an administration job in the local property agency or tourist office, or work down at the harbour, greeting tourists off the Kirkwall ferries. I was meant for this place. But not Olivia. She was different. She was special. I was ordinary.

I look up and see her again by the tree. She's facing me now and is smiling at me, gesturing with her hand for me to follow her.

She wasn't wearing that outfit on Hogmanay yet I recognize it. I remember a chilly but sunny afternoon we went walking down by the loch. We talked for two hours, our arms locked, as we always did.

We talked about Mum and Dad, school, Andy, her friends, London. She made jokes and I laughed, devouring each word, every syllable. Then later I would call Siobhan and repeat the jokes, except telling her that I made them up.

When I glance back at the tree, she's still there waiting for me. My group is a little further ahead, so I turn and start walking towards her.

'Alex?' Birkens is standing beside me, holding my arm gently. 'Alex, do you see something?'

I turn back to show him, to tell him she's right there, there's nothing to be scared of, she's safe. But she's not there any more. She never was.

*

That evening I stagger upstairs, tired, defeated. I don't know when – if – we'll ever find her. We've looked everywhere, been everywhere.

I read about a lost colony in the sixteenth century, Roanoke, in social studies last year. An entire village of men, women and children migrated to the New World to make a new life for themselves. But three years later, when a new group arrived to join them, they found no trace of the former thriving village and its inhabitants. One man lost his whole family. He searched everywhere for them, called for them, prayed for their return. But they never returned. He never saw them again.

Over four hundred years later, people still wonder where they went, if they died of disease, were killed by tribes, drowned trying to return to England. New studies suggest they just left, packed up their belongings and went to live somewhere else.

Is that what Olivia did? Did she find a new life, a new family? Or like the lost colony, will she never return, leaving us to always wonder what happened?

I don't see an answer right now. I don't know what

will happen. The search seems fruitless, a long journey where the signs to the destination begin merging into one, always telling us it's just another ten miles ahead. But no matter how far we drive, it's almost still ten miles ahead. That's how I feel, how my dad must feel. I want to stay in bed. Curl up, turn the lights off, and let the cold bitter darkness take me.

But I don't.

I get up the next morning and we look again.

Chapter Four: 04.01.2016

I've been having the same dream for three days now. It's not so much of a dream. That indicates something pleasant is happening during your REM cycle – a long-harboured ambition being realized, a new love, the meeting of two friends who haven't seen each other for a long time.

No, this isn't a dream. It's a nightmare.

I can see her, hear her. But I can't touch her. In all of my nightmares, she is always just out of reach. My mind is taunting me, playing with me. It knows I will stretch my arm out a little further to reach her. It knows I never can.

In these dreams, she is sitting on her bed, in her lavender-coloured bedroom that has photos of her and her friends on the wall in the shape of a giant letter O. In the middle of the O is a butterfly ornament, like in her real bedroom.

In the dream, I'm right there with her. I'm sitting on the rug near her, watching her dangle her legs over the side of the bed. Her toenails are painted a pale taupe and she's swinging her feet gently side to side, like windscreen wipers on a car.

Swish.

Swish.

Swish.

Then we're outside suddenly, and she's on our old swings. Again her legs hang over the edge, but here her feet can touch the ground. She's too big for the swings now. She's not a child any more.

I can feel the grass on my fingers, the tips slightly damp from the morning dew. I can smell the soil in the air from the vegetable patch where my mum had just planted strawberries the morning before. I can hear the birds overhead, squawking and communicating with each other. They're black as night. They soar overhead like my sister on the swing, gliding effortlessly through the air.

A knocking from behind makes me turn around, away from my sister. My mum's hand hammers the kitchen window. Her finger points to the sky. Her terrified screams call out to me. When I turn back, the birds aren't gliding and soaring. They're swooping. There's something different about them now. Now, they're swooping *towards* us.

Their eyes gleam like black coal and their beaks snap frantically at our clothes and hair. But I can't move. The grass grips me, its blades now sharp and suffocating. I squirm and struggle, but it won't release me. I can hear my sister screaming. I can hear her calling out to me. She's dying.

And I can't help her.

I can't reach her.

And soon, I won't be able to save her.

I beat at the ground, the blades of grass stabbing at my palm. Nails curl into the soil, heaving my body up and out from their grip. I'm dragging my body now, hurling myself towards her, trying desperately to touch her –

'Alexandra?'

I stir slightly, hearing the voice filter into my nightmare but it won't let me go.

'Alexandra?'

My eyes flicker open, and I sit upright feeling the back of the chair slam against my spine. It's over. The nightmare is over.

A deep sigh escapes my lungs and I cover my face with my hands. Why can't I shake this nightmare? Why does it follow me like this, day after day?

I look up and see DI Birkens standing over me.

'How long has she been here?' he calls out to the woman behind the glass screen in the reception room.

She shrugs her shoulders and gets back to her magazine, twirling her curly red hair with a pencil.

'How long have you been here?' he asks me.

I look at my wrist and realize I forgot to put my watch on today. I glance out of the window beside the big wooden doors that I came in. It's already beginning to get dark.

'A few hours, I think.'

He looks around. A man texts on his phone opposite us, barely glancing up. To my left, an older man sits and waits, his sheepdog curled up beside his feet. When I had come in, this place was empty. Now people wait to be noticed, wait to speak out, be heard, wait for answers to their questions. Like me.

'Is the interview room open?' he calls back towards the woman at the desk.

'No, Boyd is in there until six,' she says, not looking up.

He looks back at me and releases a long, drawn out sigh. 'Oh OK. Well, come on through.' Birkens gestures towards another set of heavy wooden doors. This one has a security keypad beside it. He punches in a four-digit code and the doors click open. He pushes them and waits for me to follow. I haven't been here since the day after my sister was officially reported missing. I had wanted to leave that day. I had thought she was just staying at a friend's house nursing a hangover. I had been so sure we'd find her. *He* had been so sure we'd find her – or had he lied to me?

I get up and hear the sheepdog barking behind me. The doors seal tight after I walk through. Dozens of desks stretch out before me, most unattended. On the desks sit stacks of file folders, coffee mugs and framed photos of smiling children.

I walk past the desks to his, wondering if these files have some new information about Olivia. I feel a dull ache spread along my shoulder blades. That chair in the waiting room was not the most comfortable. I don't remember falling asleep. I remember waiting for Birkens to come back from a call, and then being in my nightmare. It had happened so fast, before I had even felt myself slipping into sleep's grasp.

Officer Allans sees us coming and stands up from his chair. He looks eager, ambitious. All the things Detective Inspector Birkens isn't any more.

'Big night last night?' he asks Birkens.

Birkens ignores him and shakes his head. He gestures me to sit down, and walks over to a coffee cup on the windowsill.

'Don't drink that!' says Allans holding his hand out.

Birkens looks into the mug, then places it down on the desk beside me. I glance into the deep mug and see a film of white foam on the surface.

'How long has this been sitting here?' Birkens asks.

'I think you poured that cup over a week ago, sir.'

'That's disgusting,' he says. 'And stop calling me sir. It makes me feel old and superior.'

'But you are my . . . superior.'

'In a few months you'll have passed your exams and be a detective too. Then you can take over from me after I leave. You'll really have to stop calling me sir then.'

'I'll only be a DC. It'll take me years of experience to get to be you, sir. But I hope to be.'

'I hope you don't,' he says, glancing back at me.

'You're leaving?' I ask, feeling my chest tighten. He can't leave. We haven't found Olivia yet. Why would he leave now?

He sinks into a distressed brown leather chair and leans back. He legs fall to the side, and his long dark raincoat folds underneath him. I don't know why, but I want to remind him that his coat will wrinkle if he sits like that. Why did I just think of that?

Eventually he clears his throat, 'I'm retiring. Officially on the first of January but then this came up and we didn't want it to go to Aberdeen.'

I feel that pain in my chest return. I sit up and hunch over, clasping my hands together.

'Don't worry,' he says, 'I won't be going anywhere until we find your sister.'

I take a deep breath and nod, feeling a little lighter than before.

He's staying.

He'll find Olivia.

I get up from the chair and walk to the window. A seagull swoops past the glass causing me to take a step back. Seagulls are everywhere on an island. You can't escape them. Hungry, desperate birds.

'Any messages for me since I've been out?' I hear Birkens and Allans talking behind me.

'You have three phone messages from Mrs Laird. She says you promised to talk to the McAllastair boys about staying off her property. She says they're scaring the sheep again.'

'Why is it that Mrs Laird thinks I have nothing better to do with my time than tend to a sheep dispute?'

'Because we usually don't have anything better to do with our time,' laughs Allans.

I glance back at them.

'Sorry. I forgot you were here,' says Allans, his face starting to redden. 'Sir, is the interview room not free?'

I sit back in the chair and lean back, letting my knees fall awkwardly to the sides. Mahogany shelves hold books on criminal investigations, forensic evidence collections, and the odd non-fictional account of past cases from Scotland Yard. A large white board sits on the wall to the right of the bookshelf, probably meant for case profiling but a 2012 calendar is still taped to it. The office probably hadn't had a real investigation in years, clearly since before 2012. Island police crime tends to be the odd house break-in, motor vehicle theft and even an occasional sheep scaring.

I see another police officer in uniform sitting at a desk closer to the back wall, likely completing mundane administrative tasks, such as filing reports or documenting office expenses in a spreadsheet. I wonder what Glasgow's main office looks like compared to this.

The heater in the corner of the room splutters gently and churns to radiate more warmth for the office, but fails. Outside, seagulls squawk, waiting for me.

'You'll need a new calendar,' Allans says, nodding towards the white board. 'I think I have a spare one at the house. I'll get Jenn to bring it over.'

Birkens ignores him and stares at me. 'Do your parents know you're here?'

I shake my head.

He sits down beside me. 'I'll go call your mum and dad and let them know you're here. They'll be worried sick about you.'

'They probably haven't noticed I'm gone,' I mumble.

'There's nothing you can do here, Alex. We have officers out in the field following up on new leads –'

'That's a lie. You don't have any new leads,' I say.

'We'll call your house immediately if we find anything, you know that.'

'I don't want to be at home right now.'

He frowns and takes a deep breath. He looks a little younger than I first thought, maybe mid-fifties. Too young for retirement. So why is he so desperate to leave? What does he hide behind those dark eyes? He sighs and gestures to the entryway at the back of the office. 'Go make a cup of tea, and I'll call them and tell them you'll be home within a half hour. Deal?'

I nod and follow Allans to the break room. He shows me where the teabags and sugar are, and flips the kettle on for me.

He leans against the tiled counter and folds his arms against his chest. 'You know, I am really sorry that you and your family are having to go through this. It's not easy, and it's not fair.'

'Thank you.'

'My wife and I don't live too far away. If there's

anything we can ever do for your family, please let us know.'

I nod, smiling awkwardly as the churning of the kettle gets louder.

'Did your sister ever keep a diary or a journal of some kind?'

'Not sure, maybe a journal?'

He nods his head slowly.

'Why?'

'There may be something in there to indicate where she could be, who she could be with.'

'You still think she's hiding out somewhere? Even after all this?'

'She could be anywhere.'

'Not Olivia. She would see all this, the newspapers, the flyers. She's even on television. She wouldn't want us to worry like this.'

'Maybe you're right,' he says, the noise of the kettle starting to drown him out. He releases his arms, his hands dropping heavily by his side and slides past me out the door.

The break room is smaller than I thought, with only a square plastic table and five chairs around it. A fridge sits in the corner, buzzing loudly. The noise of the kettle soon masks the buzzing. It boils fast then stops.

I dunk a teabag into a chipped mug and stir milk into my tea. I'm too tired to remember where Allans said the sugar was so I drink it as is.

The heat penetrates my hands as I hold the mug in my palms. I hadn't realized how cold I was until now.

I head back towards the main office, to Birkens' desk. I can hear someone else speaking now. Another male voice, but deeper and hoarser than Birkens' or Allans'. I slow down and lean against the wall. I'm not ready to leave. I'm not ready to go home and face my parents. I rest my head and listen to them talk.

'Phonecall from Mrs Laird. You can pick it up on line two.'

I immediately recognize Birkens' voice. 'No, not today. I don't have time for her ramblings today. I have to drive Alex McCarthey to her house. Have someone take a message and tell her Davey here will get on to the McAllastair boys tomorrow.'

'No, it's not that,' says the unfamiliar voice. 'She said there's a body out by the Ring of Brodgar. Right out in the open. She said it's a girl. A dead girl.'

Suddenly the air leaves the room and I'm panting for breath. I hear my mug hitting the ground and feel hot liquid spray up my leggings. My hands are shaking wildly. What did he say?

I see Birkens in the doorway, looking at the spilled tea all around me. He looks at me, as I gasp for air. He slowly reaches his hand out to reach me, but I don't take it. I see his mouth opening, but I don't wait for his words. I just start running. I run down the hall, away from the three police officers. I hear them shouting my name, running after me.

I don't stop.

I keep going down the hallway, having no idea where I'm going. Then I see a green exit sign lit up and I know that's my way out. I slam into the door and push it open. I hear a click and the fire alarm wails.

My name is being called again, but this time it's only Birkens yelling it. I run faster, harder, until my thighs throb. I don't hear him behind me any more. He couldn't keep up.

Overgrown blades of grass strike my legs as I run through the field. The long stems tangle around my boots, and grip me, pulling me down into the soil like in my dream. But unlike in my dream, I'm stronger. I fight back and push through them, hearing them snap and break.

The earth is damp from the morning rain, and my boots sink slightly into the thick mud. It slows me down, but again I fight through.

I can still hear the police officers calling my name even though they're long gone now. Their voices echo in my head. Then I hear Olivia's. She's screaming, like in my dream.

I can't help her.

I can't reach her.

Olivia, I'm coming.

Wait for me.

I know exactly where I'm going and I know I've reached it by the crowds of people gathered. Their bodies block the standing stones and I can't see past them. Two police cars with flashing lights are parked horizontally, and officers frantically tape off the car park, shouting to the crowd to move back. But they don't move. They strain their necks to see more. They're enjoying this, I think. They like the drama, the excitement in the air. They crave it. They're bored. They are here because they need this.

I start pushing them out of the way, hearing them swear at me. A couple of them turn and see my face and nudge their friends. They recognize me. They all think exactly what I'm thinking – that's my sister out there. My sister's body has been found.

She's dead.

I push them harder, screaming at them, 'Move!' My body hits the yellow tape and I see a female office running towards me. 'Stop!' she yells. But I don't. I can't.

I duck under the tape and start running again, this time faster. Another officer starts chasing me, but he can't reach me.

The slick grass is harder to run on, and it slows me down. I see two officers standing over something. It's long, and it lays awkwardly on the ground. I see an arm. A leg. Long dark brown hair spread wide on the grass.

Suddenly I feel arms around me, pulling me away, pulling me down. I hear Birkens' voice trying to calm me but I thrash violently. 'Let me go!' I scream. The officers ahead turn at the noise and that's when I see her more clearly.

My sister. My big sister. That's me lying there. That's my blood. We share the same blood. And it's everywhere. It's all around her head. It's on the grass, it's matted in her hair.

Then everything goes blurry. I grip Birkens' shoulder and throw my head back. I see birds soaring overhead, circling us, circling her. I open my mouth and scream my sister's name. Then darkness takes me.

Chapter Five: 24.10.2015

Olivia

I met him at my school. He's a little taller than me, with dark hair and even darker eyes. But there's a kindness to them too. He wants people to know only the character he performs. And most people only see that, only *want* to see that.

But not me.

I see him for who he is, who he really wants to be. And he's so much more than that character.

We all play characters to a certain extent. We're all pieces in a game, moved by hands not always ours. And we play our roles well. We do what people expect us to do, say what they want us to say, even if that means lying. Because the truth is so much harder to hear for most people.

I played the game for too long. But I can't any more. I'm so tired of it. I want to make my own decisions now, play by my own rules. Even if that means hurting people, many of them people I loved at some point in the game.

I feel the worst when I think about hurting James. I

don't want to hurt him, but I can't keep up the facade any longer. He's kind, he's sweet to me, he's been a good friend. But I've met someone. And he's different. I feel different when I'm around him. I don't feel like the character I play. I feel like me.

My friends noticed him too. They made comments to me, and nudged me when he walked past. I smiled, he smiled back. And when I passed him, I turned back to see if he was still watching. And he was.

I didn't see him again for ages after that first time. I don't know why. I looked around the school for him, out onto the street, down to the beach in case he walked there, down the big hill to see the ferries come in from Isle of Graemsay or Moaness. But he wasn't there. He wasn't anywhere.

Then one day, I saw him again. And after that I saw him every day.

We would hang out after school, get coffee from The Gallery Coffee Shop in Kirkwall where no one recognized us. You know, the kind of coffee that comes in a little to-go waxed paper cup, and we would sit on the beach away from Stromness, away from the big hill so no one saw us. I would bundle up and stick my hands in my pocket, and he would gently take my hands and hold them between his to warm them up. I would giggle, he would smile. And we did that most days for the first month.

We would talk for hours before I had to leave to pick up my sister from her friend's. I wouldn't want to leave so when I did, I would be a little angry at my sister for making me do it. I know it wasn't her fault. She didn't know. She would have just walked or taken a bus or asked Siobhan's mum for a lift home, if only she knew. But she didn't. He asked me not to tell anyone, not my sister or my friends, and I won't betray his trust like that.

And I don't think they or she would understand. They will judge me, without hearing the whole truth. They won't listen to me, not like he does. Only he listens.

He listens to everything I have to say, not just the important stuff. When I talk, his eyes are on me and he's absorbing every word, every syllable that leaves my lips. I didn't know I liked to talk so much until I met someone who liked to listen.

I wish we could go for dinner or see a movie at the cinema together like a normal couple, but we can't. And that's OK, I guess. Because what we do, our little moments together, is enough for me. And I'd rather that than nothing at all.

He's seen me dance. He snuck into the Autumn Dance Showcase and saw my performance. I knew he was coming so I had time to be nervous.

Butterflies fluttered furiously in my belly right up until the curtain was raised. Then the lights dimmed, the music started, and everything went away. All I was left with was the rhythm of the music and my body – the instrument.

I had practised my choreography for weeks. Everyone in the audience had seen me dance at some point, everyone except him. Besides, it's different when you dance for the person you love.

Did I just say that?

Yes, I guess I did.

I love him.

I don't know when that started, but somehow I've found myself right in the middle, not even realizing that it had begun.

It's too late now.

I saw James yesterday. He still wants to talk about why we broke up. I just don't have anything left to say to him. He was my friend before he was my boyfriend, and I really want him to be my friend again. Me, him, Em, we were inseparable at one time. We did everything together, went everywhere, shared everything.

But it's not realistic to expect everything to stay the same. Because people grow up. They aren't the same. They change. I've changed. And so have my feelings towards him.

But I want my friend back. I never said goodbye to him, just the relationship that had blossomed from the friendship. I want to go back to where we started.

I guess change scares me a little too.

But when it comes to the future, I need change. I need to break free of this place, of this character I've moulded into.

I haven't told him yet about London. I don't know how to tell him. It's still so new. I enjoy spending time with him. I love him, but I can't stay here for him.

There's so much I still want to do with my life, so much I want to see. With James, it was so easy. But with him, it's different, not so easy. I can tell him anything, but I can't tell him what to do, what to feel.

He's going to want me to stay, I know he is. He can't come with me. He has too much here. He sacrificed everything for his last relationship. But that's over now. I can't ask him to sacrifice all over again. This is supposed to be a new beginning for us both.

I want him to come with me. But I can't say those words. His answer might devastate us.

Because if he doesn't come, I won't stay.

I know my little sister Alex doesn't get it, why I want to leave so badly. It's not that I hate it here. She thinks it is. She thinks it's too small for me. It is a small island, but it's not too small for me. I just have this fire in my stomach to go. I want to start in London, dance. Then I want to travel around the world. I want to see it all, and not miss one moment.

I want to go to Switzerland, Italy, France. I want to kiss a stranger in New York City in Times Square like in the old photo of a sailor from the 1940s. I want to take a surfing lesson in Australia. I want to explore a sulphur cave in New Zealand, and ride a camel in Morocco. I want to walk along the Great Wall of China, watch the sun set in Hawaii, ride in a cable car up to Sugar Loaf

Mountain in Brazil. I want to scream as loud as my lungs can cope over the Grand Canyon.

My sister is always talking about the flower that blooms just once at midnight – the kadapul flower, which is only found in Sri Lanka. When I told her I'd go there and pick it for her, she laughed and said I couldn't, because it withers almost as soon as you pick it. And when I told her she should go there then to see it in person she laughed even harder.

My sister will never leave this island.

And she seems to be OK with that.

I don't get it. We're so different in that regard. But I guess she knows what makes her happy. I just hope she'll come visit me in London.

London.

I don't know how to tell him about London.

I'm not ready to say goodbye to him yet. But I'm not willing to say goodbye to my dreams either.

I dream about stepping on to that aeroplane. I've never been on a plane before. The furthest I've ever been to is Aberdeen, and we took the ferry.

Sometimes I lie in bed and think about being up in the air in that plane. Passport in hand, bag beside me, watching Orkney fade into the distance. Knowing that when I return – and I will return – that I would have explored the world, seen so much, felt so much.

That plane will soar so high in the sky, and for the first time I will feel free.

Free as a bird.

Chapter Six: 04.01.2016

I hear noises in the fog, calling to me, beckoning me out of the dark. I feel lost, confused about whether I'm awake or sleeping. I'm dreaming because I see shapes and shadows. They merge together and form new configurations, but none of them are familiar or comforting.

Somewhere in the fog, I see hair. Brown strands weave in and out, flowing like a gentle ocean wave. I reach out and feel the strands touch my fingertips, but it feels damp, sticky. When I release my fingers, letting the hair drop and flow back into the dense greyness, a red residue remains on my skin. Rubbing my fingers together, it spreads down my skin and to my wrists. It's warm, thick, and moves like a snake twisting and coiling its way up my arm.

I open my mouth to scream, but it's too fast. The liquid is inside me, filling my cheeks. It's then I realise that it's not hair, it's blood, and the veins are moving like they're alive within me.

The fog thickens, the voices getting louder, stronger. They break through the blanket of emptiness and pull me from its grasp. A jolt hits me, and a hardness cups my body. I feel heavy, but empty at the same time. A low buzzing fills the air around me, and I feel myself sinking. I know now I'm not awake, because my limbs start to come alive, wakening and pushing my mind out of the deep slumber.

A throbbing sensation fills my body, and targets my head. I feel warm, too warm. A stream of lighting pinches at my eyes as I slowly blink them open. Where am I?

I open them wide, and see Birkens sitting in a chair. He's slumped with his elbow propped and his chin resting on his hand. A small pendant or keyring dangles from his right hand. It looks like a figure in a red cloak. A superhero of some kind. Superman. He holds a Superman keyring in his hand but I don't know why. He's not moving. At first I think he's sleeping but as my vision clears, sharpening everything around me, I can see his eyes are open and he's looking at me. His eyes are slightly glazed, and his jaw is tensed. He looks like my dad when he's worried about something.

Dad.

Mum.

Who's going to tell them? Or maybe they already know.

'Where am I?' I ask.

'You're at Balfour Hospital.'

'What happened?'

'You collapsed. I was worried.'

Suddenly it all comes rushing back – the standing stones, the body, the birds. My back arches as I bite my lip to stop myself from crying out again. I put my hand over my face so he can't see me cry. But the tears don't come. Instead, I feel empty. As if my body can't grieve any more. But it shakes as if it's still crying.

I feel his hand on my hand. 'It's OK. Alex, it's OK.'

I move my hand. 'Where are my parents?'

'They're at the station. We needed a positive ID on the body so we know for sure it's your sister.'

I don't say anything. I don't know what to say. 'The body.' My sister was just that now: a body. Nothing more. An empty vessel. Has her soul really left her body, or does any part of her remain in that shell?

Is she gone?

Olivia.

I see her eyes. Wide. Open. Vacant. Hot bile rises up my throat. I throw my head over the hospital bed and start vomiting on the floor. I'm not even ashamed or embarrassed.

Birkens starts calling for the nurse. She rushes in and grabs a basin from the corner of the room and places it underneath me. I feel her cold hands scoop up my hair and brush it gently from my face. I close my eyes and feel a cool washcloth on my face. I lie back and allow her to pat my face over and over again until I feel the fire in my body die down, only left to flicker.

'I'm sorry,' I stutter, feeling my lungs fill with heat.

'Don't be sorry. Your body is reacting to the shock,' says Birkens.

I feel my breathing slow to a normal pace. My body feels heavy, tired.

'Alex, I need to ask you about the night of the thirty-first again.' He stops, waiting for my reaction, then continues, 'You said your sister left the house after dinner, that it was around quarter to seven in the evening. Can you be sure that was the time?'

'I don't know . . . I think so?'

'Do you remember what she was wearing?'

'A top and jeans.'

'What kind of top?'

'I don't remember.'

'Was it a jumper? A hoodie?'

'She wasn't really a hoodie type.' That was more *my* style.

'OK, then a vest thing with straps?'

'Yeah, it was sleeveless. And sparkly.'

'Silver?'

'Yes, and she wore it with her necklace, the one she has on all the time.'

'What did the necklace look like?'

'It's gold, with a thin chain.'

'Did it have a pendant?'

'The letter O . . . can I have it, you know, when you're done with the . . . um . . . body? I'd like to keep it, if that's OK. I think she'd want me to have it.'

I feel that ache coming back in my belly.

'She wasn't wearing a necklace when we found her,' says Birkens, writing down something on his pad.

'Oh, that's odd. She always wears it, and I'm pretty certain she left the house with it.'

'Pretty certain?'

'Very certain.'

He nods and keeps writing.

'Can you find it?' I ask him.

He drops his pen and looks up at me. 'Of course, I know how important it is.'

Nodding my head, I picture her sitting at the dining table. Her elbows are resting on the dark mahogany. The fork swings mindlessly from her fingers, circling above the plate. She's not hungry. Her roast chicken sits getting cold, as her carrots lay limp beside the buttered potatoes. Her other hand is woven into her long hair, the strands twirling around her index finger. Mum is telling her that our cousin Karin is pregnant again, and that our next-door neighbour Lillian just bought a new car. She's listening and smiling, but it's not her smile. There's something different about her tonight. She seems anxious, like she's thinking about other things. Like she's worried about something.

She glances my way, and I immediately smile. The corners of her mouth turn up and for a moment she relaxes. She gestures towards Mum and rolls her eyes. I cover my mouth and stifle a laugh. Mum does tend to talk your ear off when she's excited about something.

They're going out tonight with their friends. They never go out. Mum is wearing a new dress, and has styled her curly auburn hair with a little hairspray. Even Dad's dressed up a little. Everyone's going out, except me. Andy and Siobhan will be here soon.

There's excitement in the air, I can feel it. Tomorrow's a new day, a fresh start for us. Anything can happen tonight. I might even tell Andy how I really feel.

Andy.

Siobhan.

I'm suddenly back in the hospital room, my last memory of her fading.

How do you tell your best friends that your sister's been murdered? What do I expect them to say?

'Alex?'

Birkens is looking at me like he's just said something. He's waiting.

'What did you say?'

'What did you talk about that night?'

'I think I told you all this – school, friends. Mum was telling us about our cousin.'

He shifts forward, leaning closer into me, and bows his head slightly like he's thinking about what to ask next.

'She seemed worried at dinner,' I say, watching as his head pops up quickly.

'Worried? How?'

'I don't know. I was just thinking about that evening, and she seemed a little quieter than usual.'

'How was she acting?'

'Fidgety? She seemed to be elsewhere at the table while we talked. I thought maybe she was bored at the time but now I'm not so sure. Now I think she was worried about something.'

'That's good. You're beginning to remember things, question things. That's what will help us in the investigation.'

The door clicks open and Allans is standing in the doorway, his hands in his pockets. He nods to Birkens who nods back, words apparently not needed between two colleagues. I wonder if there has been any new information since I woke, if he has just seen my parents, if he was the one who had to pull back the sheet on my sister's body to expose her face and watch how they responded.

Birkens should have been the one to do it. They know him best. He's the one in charge of this whole investigation. He's the one who promised us that he would find her. He's the one who failed us.

But he couldn't. He's here with me, because I was weak and collapsed. He felt responsible and now I'm here taking up precious investigation time. Maybe I'm the one who failed us.

'I'm very sorry,' Allans says, glancing awkwardly at me as he shifts closer to the hospital bed. He looks scared, timid, like he's approaching a wild, unpredictable animal.

I'm not going to break. I can handle this. I think.

'Alex, did your sister say anything to you before she left? Can you remember the last thing she said to you?'

I look down at my fingers as they fidget with the blanket on my bed. Squeezing the fabric in my hand, voices in the corridor get louder. The hospital seems busy today. The light beams in from the window, making my eyes sting a little.

'I don't remember,' I finally say. 'I don't remember the last thing I said to her, or that she said to me.'

My eyes sting more, this time with hot tears. How could I not remember my last moments with my sister?

I grit my teeth until my jaw aches. 'Why are you asking me all this? Why now?' I cry.

'I'm sorry, Alex. I know this isn't a good time to be asking these questions. But it's imperative that we nail down the timeline of events.'

'I can't think right now.' I rest my head down on the pillow, feeling the cool fabric slide against my cheek.

Birkens stands up, puts his coat on and starts towards Allans, gesturing him out the door.

'Are you leaving now?'

'I have to get back to the station. Your mum and dad should be on their way.'

'No, I mean are you leaving? You know, retiring now?'

He stops and turns back, his large frame blocking the light from the doorway. 'No, why would I leave now?'

'You said you'd stay until we found my sister. Well, we found her.' I feel my lip tremble and scold myself for sounding like a bitter sarcastic teenager. I want him to see me as more than that. I want him to see me as an adult. I'm sick of people treating me like a child all the time. I'm not a child any more. Even if I was this morning, I'm not now. Not after seeing that. Any childhood I had, has now been stripped away, leaving me in the cold to find my own way home.

'This wasn't what I had expected,' he says.

'Yes it is. Even Allans said after forty-eight hours, the chances of finding her alive are significantly reduced.'

Birkens looks ahead and I wonder if Allans is beyond the door. He turns back, his jaw a little stiff. 'He didn't mean to say that.'

'You both knew. Maybe everyone knew, except me.'

He turns to leave.

'Bye then,' I say, closing my eyes, blocking him out.

'I'm not leaving, Alex. I'm going to find who did this.' He walks out, letting the light from the hallway push back in again.

I sit up and watch him walk down the hallway, his coat swaying behind him as he marches alongside Allans, past nurses and doctors and hospital equipment.

'I'm going to find who did this.' Why would he say that?

Someone did this?

Of course. This wasn't an accident. Someone is to blame for this.

I can't even think the words let alone believe them.

I can't. I can't say this.

This can't be real.

My sister was *murdered*.

Chapter Seven: 05.01.2016

It's still dark outside my window. The sun won't rise until closer to nine o'clock. That means for the next two hours, my house and all of Orkney will be completely veiled in darkness. That's how I feel anyway. Consumed by darkness.

It's my birthday on the 11th, six days from now.

I don't know why I just thought about that.

I don't care for my birthday anyway. Another year getting older. But for Olivia, it was another year closer to finishing school and moving away from Orkney. For Olivia, birthdays were special. Not for me.

She won't be here this year. Or next. Or ever. She'll never wish me happy birthday again.

And I'll never be able to wish her a happy birthday again. Hers is the 8th of October. Her birthstone is opal. I know because I bought her a keyring with an opal pendant on it from the chemist for her birthday last year. Mine is garnet, which I hate. I don't like the colour red. I wish it was opal like Olivia's.

Throwing the covers off, I walk over to my window and look out. The moon is still high and bright. A couple of lights flicker in the sky. There are very few ways to get on this island, and even fewer ways to get off.

I need to get out. I need some air. I can't be in this house right now.

I skip a shower and dress quickly instead, layering and bundling as much as I can. My feet tiptoe down the stairs, steps softened by the carpet. When I reach the bottom, the flooring creaks slightly. The kitchen light is still on. Someone's up early, or they never went to bed at all.

I creep past the living room door, and see my dad sitting on the sofa staring out. The TV is off, the radio is off. He's just sitting there, staring.

I want to say something, I do. But I can't.

He reminds me so much of her. And I probably remind him of her.

I want to hug him. I want him to hug me. But I also want to hit him. He lied to me. He told me we'd find her. He told me she would call. She didn't. She's not fine. And she couldn't call. She's dead.

Why do adults lie to us? Because we're fragile and might break? Too late. I'm already broken. And there's no way of putting me back together, not completely anyway.

I step back and head out of the backdoor, through the garden. Even if he hears me, he doesn't come after me. He doesn't try and stop me, tell me to stay inside because he's scared of losing another daughter. He doesn't hug me, tell me he's sorry for lying to me, sorry for promising that everything would be fine when no one can really promise that. No, no one comes after me. No one cares. Because we're not fine. Nobody's fine.

The buses have already started running, they start early. I pull the woollen hat down over my forehead, down to my eyes, and keep my head down. I mutter to the driver and don't look at him, in case he recognizes me. I don't feel like talking to anyone today. I don't feel like answering any questions, or getting any looks of pity from anyone.

Today I just want to be left alone.

The road is slick, so we drive slowly. Houses tucked safely behind stone walls pass by, some with lights on, some in darkness still. I wonder how many got up this morning to turn on the news or pick up the newspaper from their doormat beneath their letterbox, only to find their fears confirmed. Yes, there's a killer on this island. Someone out there has murdered a girl. My sister. Lock your doors, put up your little fences, don't walk home alone. You could be next.

I touch my forehead to the cold glass and close my eyes. I didn't sleep at all last night. I'd rested my head down on my pillow and just stared at the wall in front of me. Bit like my dad, I suppose.

I'm tired, but I can't close my eyes. I'm scared of the nightmares that wait for me.

When the bus reaches the bottom of the B9055, I push the stop button and step out from the side door.

As it drives away, I slide my hood down and fix my hat so I can see out.

A thin mist shrouds the shoreline, as I walk up the winding road past the looming Standing Stones of Stenness, back to the Ring of Brodgar. I know I shouldn't return but I have to, just one more time.

No.

Feelings from the day before flood back. Now I'm on the ground, on my knees, my fingers digging into the cold ground and gripping the soil.

I can't breathe.

Gasping for air, I remember why I came and slowly rise to my feet again. Stumbling, I make my way back there. Oxygen flows in and out but I still don't feel it in my lungs. A small sound escapes my lips as I see the stones rising from the ground.

I see her empty eyes again. The blood around her hairline. The arm stretched out, like she'd been reaching for something, or someone.

I'm on the ground again. My back spasms as I heave in and out. I close my eyes so hard, it hurts my whole face. Warm tears stream down my cheeks and I wipe them away roughly with the back of my glove.

When I rise again, I notice all of the cars. Most are police, but some look like everyday cars. Yellow and black tape curls around the entire area and metal fences are set up around the stone where Olivia was found. Police officers walk around, some with small clear plastic bags in their hands, others with notepads and pens.

They're collecting evidence. But what they are seeing? Do they know who killed my sister?

There's so many of them. I didn't know Orkney had this many police officers, unless some came from Aberdeen. Or maybe Birkens called some of his old friends from Edinburgh to come and help.

A small group of people in regular clothing stand near the entrance barrier, on the other side of the tape, armed with notepads and pens. They reach their arms out when a police officer walks by and try to get their attention, but the officers ignore them. Some are frantically taking photos. One of them is standing in front of a big camera and talking with a microphone to the screen. They're reporters, all of them. Here to get the next big story. Well, they found it.

Then I see Detective Inspector Birkens. He's the only one standing inside the metal fencing. He's squatting near where she was found. He's wearing gloves, but not the kind that I have on. These are rubbery white gloves, like a doctor or nurse wears in the hospital.

He glances up and for a moment I think he sees me. But he doesn't wave or gesture to me, he keeps his head down.

My feet back up, and I begin to turn away. I can't get down there today. I'll have to come back, if I can. I need to be there. I need to touch the stone where she lay. I need to touch the last thing she touched.

I take the long way, needing more time, more air. By the time I get back to the house, there's a car in the driveway. At first I think it's new then I remember I've seen it here before. I think it's that detective's car.

When I open the front door, my dad immediately rushes to me. 'Where have you been? I went upstairs to your bedroom and found your bed empty! Have you any idea how scared I was? How could you be so . . . so . . .' His eyes water, and I take a step back.

'I'm sorry. I didn't mean to worry you. I just needed to go for a walk,' I say, sliding out of my coat and gloves. 'Is someone here?'

He nods and goes into the living room. I follow him and find Birkens sitting on the sofa. He's alone today.

'Hello Alexandra . . . sorry, Alex.' He's cradling a mug in his hands.

I smile weakly and go to sit down beside my dad.

He leans in and addresses my dad. 'Perhaps, Mr McCarthey, your daughter can go upstairs. This really isn't information she should be hearing at this age.'

My dad turns to me but before he can speak, I blurt out, 'Dad, please. I need to know what's going on. I'm in this too. Besides, I'm probably going to read about it in the newspapers tomorrow anyway.'

My dad and the detective exchange glances in some kind of unspoken language. The detective nods, and continues, 'I've assigned a family liaison officer to you. She'll be checking in with you in the next day or so.'

'What for?' asks my dad.

'She's trained to work with families who have recently lost a loved one, to be a liaison between the police and the family, to gather information, to share information –'

'Can't you do that?' I ask.

'I'm going to be looking for the person responsible for Olivia's death. So no, I can't do that. But I will be checking in myself as much as I can.'

'Has there been any news?' My dad leans in, desperate for something, even a crumb of new information that allows us to get one step closer to the truth.

'We're still doing preliminary forensics, but initial findings indicate that Olivia died in that location within the last day or so. We'd need to complete an autopsy –'

'What's that?' I ask.

'It's a post-mortem examination of the body to gather more information on time of death, and of course, to determine a cause of death. We can also check for DNA left behind from whoever did this – hair follicles, skin cells, fluids –'

'Do you do this?' I have so many questions. How does this work? It's not like we were prepared for it at all.

'No, not me. It needs to be a medical professional that specializes in autopsies. We have a pathologist coming in from Aberdeen this afternoon, but we need you to sign some paperwork first.'

'Of course,' mutters my dad. He's trembling slightly. He looks like he's going to be sick.

'Are you OK? Would you like to have this conversation another time?' Birkens asks.

'No. Please continue. Alex, are you OK?'

I loop my hand through my dad's arm and lean in to him slightly. 'I'm OK. Go on.'

'There was some disturbance on the soil around the soles of her feet and around her hands. Her shoes were removed. And we also have her car.'

'You found her car?' my dad repeats slowly, as if he needs more time to process that last piece of information.

'Yes, it was found near the scene. It's been wiped down, but we're checking it thoroughly for DNA.'

'It's a tourist attraction,' my dad says. 'Thousands of people come here each year to visit the Ring of Brodgar.'

'Yes,' nods Birkens.

'No, I mean, there must be cameras or something so police can keep an eye on it to make sure it doesn't get vandalised or graffitied on, right?'

'There are no cameras by the standing stones –'

'What about the car park?'

'Yes, we've checked those already. Whoever did this smashed out all of the screens on the cameras. We have no security footage from the last three nights.'

'What does this mean?' I ask.

'It means that whoever did this knew what he was doing.'

Chapter Eight: 06.01.2016

When I wake, I hear his words in my head. 'Whoever did this knew what he was doing.'

What does that even mean? Is this someone that's killed before? Someone who has taken a life with his own hands at another time?

My hands hide my face, but my touch feels unfamiliar. My skin feels numb. Everything seems to be moving in slow motion around me.

When I rise, I see the rooftops are dusted with a thin veil of snow. I wonder what people are doing right now. I can't imagine living a normal life now. It seems so foreign to me.

When I step into the hallway, my parents' bedroom door is open. My mum's back is to me. She's sitting up on the bed, but she doesn't look like she's showered or dressed. When I get closer, she's holding a framed photo of Olivia in her hands. She's gripping the wooden frame so tight that her knuckles are white.

'Mum?'

She turns around and drops the frame. She looks confused, scared maybe. It's like she doesn't recognize me, or understand why I'm still here, when Olivia is gone. Why I survived and she didn't.

'Do you want a cup of tea?'

She turns her back away from me and picks up the photo, cradling it again in her hands. 'No. No, thank you.'

Dad's in the kitchen. He's standing against the counter cradling the newspaper, like Mum is doing with the frame. Both have Olivia's face.

He glances up towards Olivia's bedroom as if he can still hear her up there.

It's cold in here. Bitter. Icy.

Someone must have left a window open. I go into the living room and kneel down in front of the wood stove. I drag the basket over, and start layering the kindling and large chunks of wood in a heap, criss-crossing them like Dad showed me. Then I pull out old newspaper and start tearing the pages and scrunching them into thin strips. I slide the strips in to fill the holes between the kindling and the larger pieces of wood.

I need more. My fingers graze the bottom of the empty basket so I start walking through the house to find more paper. I see a stack beside the sofa so I pick up the top one.

I see her.

There she is, on the front of the newspaper again. 'Local Girl Dead.' They used a new photo of her this time. She's standing in front of the school with her arms stretched out, advertising the Autumn Dance

Showcase. She wears a beige cardigan and a tan still fresh from her holiday to Spain. She'd saved up her earnings from working in the bakery last year and gone away with her mates. I remember how excited she was. She couldn't wait to get off the island. She hated living here – a rural, isolated existence, she called it. She had come back raving about Spain and how she loved that no one knew her over there. It made her more excited for London.

She wanted to travel everywhere and anywhere. Now she'd never leave this island. She was born here, and she died here. Once we bury her, it would be final. Her bones and flesh would become a part of this island's soil and it would never release her. She would never be free.

Dropping the paper and lighter, I run down the hall to my bedroom. Tears fall down my cheeks, soaking me in my own grief. I can barely breathe. Gasping for air, I open the door to her room instead of mine. Pushing it open, a stark cold breeze meets me at the doorway, chilling my bones.

Detective Inspector Birkens is in there. He's sitting on her bed.

He quickly rises at the sight of me. 'Sorry, I just wanted to have another look in your sister's bedroom. We're still searching for her phone.'

'Oh, how did you get in?'

'Your dad let me in.'

I'm in my pyjamas still. My eyes are still moist from my tears, and my face is probably red and splotchy.

'I'm all done in here,' he says, starting to leave.

'I can't stop thinking about what you said. About this person knowing what they were doing.'

'I'm sorry, Alexandra. I didn't mean to scare you.'

'I'm not a child. You didn't scare me. I'm just wondering, do you think it was planned? Do you think this person intended to kill my sister and had been thinking about doing it for days, maybe even weeks?'

He starts towards me, but I can't stop.

'My dad left the door unlocked that night. He never does lock that stupid door. He used to joke that we have nothing of value to steal. And my mum said she was going to wait up for Olivia until she got home. But she fell asleep on the sofa, and didn't wake until it was morning. That's when she noticed Olivia hadn't come home. And me? I was supposed to call her if she was running late. She said she'd be back at ten to watch a movie with me, and I assumed she'd forgotten and I didn't care. I was angry at her because I thought she was having more fun with her friends and didn't want to come home. I could have called her . . . I should have called her. But I didn't. Instead, I was engrossed in a stupid news story about birds falling from the sky again in America.'

'You're wondering if there was anything you or anyone else could have done to stop this.'

'No, I'm wondering if we let this happen, or worse, caused this.'

'It's nobody's fault. No one's to blame. Horrible things

happen sometimes, and you have to . . . release yourself from the guilt.' He doesn't sound like he believes his own words. Does he too carry guilt with him?

'I'll give you some time,' he says as he walks out. He's holding the Superman keyring again, but this time it looks like he's squeezing it, or stroking it or something. Why does he always have that? What is it?

I watch him leave, hear his feet on the stairs as he descends, feel the vibrations of his deep voice under my feet as he converses with my dad directly below me.

I'm alone in her bedroom now.

But I suddenly don't want to be here any more. I can't stay in here. So I leave.

In the time that it takes me to change, the phone rings six times and the doorbell chimes three times. Everyone wants a piece of the story, a new headline for tomorrow's paper.

As far as I know, my parents haven't talked to anyone. DI Birkens released a statement shortly after Olivia was found, asking the press to be 'respectful' of the family and 'give them the space to grieve'. He had also added later, 'We'll know who did this soon enough. There will be justice for Olivia McCarthey.'

I'm still waiting for that justice.

A noise at my bedroom window startles me, but I ignore it and go back to getting ready.

There it is again.

It sounds like a small stone or pebble being thrown at my window.

Sliding the window open, instantly blasted with cold air, I find Andy standing in the garden waving at me among a sea of cameras, journalists and police officers. It's a circus out there.

I gesture round the back of the house and go down to meet him.

I don't know why he's here. I'm not answering the phone, or talking to anyone right now. Like Birkens said, we just need space to grieve. That includes space from our own lives and those in it.

I slide on my thick coat and gloves, unlock the back door – we lock our doors now – and slip outside to meet him in the back garden.

He's shivering, kicking at the cold ground. He turns to see me and smiles. His arms are around me, and he's hugging me but I can't feel anything. This all feels so strange now.

His smile fades, and his eyes burn into me. 'Why didn't you call?' he asks, dropping his arms.

'And say what?'

'That they found your sister?'

'How can you say what happened over a phone call?'

'Then you should have come round.'

'Why? You would have found out about Olivia on the news.'

'But I wanted to find out from you. We're –'

We're what? We never got to that stage yet. We had shared a kiss at New Year, after months of just hanging out. I had been so happy. I had thought about doing it for weeks before it finally happened. But then everything changed. And so did I. So did we.

We're not anything any more.

I don't even who I am any more.

'Come out with us tonight. My older brother is going to buy us beer and cider, and we can go hang out at the park behind the academy. Forget about all this for a night.'

I couldn't forget, even if I wanted to. Which I don't. Not right now, anyway. Not when the killer is still out there. I'm needed here. Here I can help. Here I have a purpose.

'I'm not allowed out after dark, and you shouldn't be either,' I finally say.

'Alex, come on. It's almost your birthday.'

'I don't really feel like celebrating,' I snap.

'I didn't mean –'

'I should go back in. Thanks for stopping over, Andy. Have fun tonight.'

I close the door quickly before he can say anything else to confirm the distance between us.

Chapter Nine: 07.01.2016

My feet touch the top step and as I reach for my bedroom door, a flicker of movement turns my head.

Olivia's door is slightly ajar, an ember glow spreading out from the crack and stretching out towards my feet.

Closing my eyes I can hear her music playing softly from under the door. I don't know what it is, but I like it. She always found artists that I'd never heard of before. And they always became my favourite band or singer for that day. I'd listen to the song over and over again. And the next day, when she introduced me to a new one, I'd become obsessed with that one. Truth is, she could have shown me anything, and I would have loved it. The mere fact that she liked it made me love it.

Eyes still closed, I move closer to her door. The wood is cold beneath my fingers, the white paint flaking slightly. I smell the juniper scent of her candle wafting through the crack in the door. It's the candle I bought her for her birthday. The scent is strong, like pine needles, lemon and tart berries. I'd recited a passage from my botany encyclopedia about the medicinal effects of juniper berries and how people back in the day would burn them to control epidemics that swept through their vulnerable villages.

Olivia was always so patient. She nodded, and often asked me questions, but I could tell her mind was elsewhere. In her mind, she saw movement, rhythm, and multi-syllabic notes. In mine, I saw the earth – flat, smooth, filled with wondrous smells and beauty. My mind was stationary, while hers wandered free. She saw the forest. I saw but one tree.

Occasionally when she threw me a rope, she pulled me into her world, to her way of seeing things. And although it was magnificent, even more so to be closer to her, to understand her more, I always knew in the end that it was not my world. Mine was much less vast than hers, much more . . . methodical.

The sound of her giggling as she gossips with Emily about what happened at school that day pulls me back in. And when I creep closer and take a look inside, I see her lying on the bed on her belly with the phone in one hand, and her other fingers playing with the fabrics of her blanket. She scoops up the wool, squeezing it in her palm as she gasps along with whatever dramatic story Emily is telling her. And when she laughs, she releases the blanket and throws her hand to her mouth. Sometimes I'd catch her eye when I looked in, and a wide smile would stretch across her face. Sometimes she'd wave. Other times – those special times – she'd beckon me in closer, wanting me to sit beside her while she braided my hair and finished her conversation. This close, I'd hear Emily's voice too, and for a moment I'd feel like I was one of them, a part of the gang, a part of their friendship.

But this time when I push open the door, I only see my mum sitting on Olivia's bed.

I don't see her.

And there's no music playing. No juniper candle sparking and flickering. No warmth from the bedside lamp. No warmth from anywhere.

'Mum?'

She startles and looks up at me, momentarily confused about who this person standing before her is. I open my mouth to say, 'It's me. It's Alex.' But her pupils focus and she forces a smile in my direction.

'Oh, hi. You scared me.'

'Sorry. I saw her bedroom door open.'

'Yeah, I come in here sometimes,' she says, tilting her head back to take in the whole room, and everything it contains, or once contained.

'Me too.'

I sit beside her on the bed, and feel the shift in the mattress. I then notice she's holding a photo of Olivia dancing. Her body is in mid-air, legs stretched out, fabrics of her dress lifted around her thighs.

'Why do you think she became a dancer?' I ask, tapping the photo with my finger.

My mum smiles and strokes the edges of the picture with her thumb. 'I think she danced because I did. It's in our blood.'

up, straightens her dress and looks around as if she can't remember what she came in here for.

'I should start dinner. Your dad will be home soon. Please don't touch anything in here.'

And just like that, the small window that opened up for me to climb through closes.

I return to my own bedroom after she leaves, and close the door behind me.

Her words linger in my mind, and I close my eyes to stop the tears from falling. I collapse on my bed and pull the covers in towards my chin. It's too early to sleep, too dark to face the day.

My dad lost his best friend that night. My mum lost a piece of her that night. I know what I lost. But what is left behind? What do I have to offer my mum and dad? I'm not her.

The wrong person died that night.

And everyone is thinking that.

'You danced?'

She nods, her eyes never leaving the photo.

'You never told me that. Did Olivia know?'

'She found some old photos that Gran took of me at a ballet class. She kept one of them.'

'Oh, she never showed me,' I say, my voice exposing the disappointment. This was a piece of Mum that I never knew, a piece that my sister kept from me. Why would she do that?

'Olivia was already starting to show an interest in dance at that point, so I encouraged her. She reminded me so much of myself at that age. And she was good. Oh my god, she was good at it.'

'Yeah, she was.'

'She danced better than I ever could. She danced like she didn't care about anything. She was so brave in her dancing. I always felt like I held back.'

'What happened? Why did you stop?'

'I met your father.'

'How?'

'We met in the pub and that was that. I fell pregnant with Olivia shortly after and our families encouraged us to get married.'

'Oh.' Was this not the life Mum wanted? Had she not wanted to marry my dad?

'Don't get me wrong, I loved your father very much. Marrying him was the best thing I ever did. It gave me two beautiful daughters.' She wraps her arm around me and squeezes slightly.

'But you had to give up your dancing?'

'I thought after I had Olivia, I could get back into it but my body had changed. It just didn't respond the way it did before. It had given up on that life, and after a while, so did I.'

'What would have happened had you not met Dad?'

'I can't think like that, honey.'

'But if you had to, what would have happened?'

'Well, I had a place with a dance company in Edinburgh. We were about to train for the Edinburgh International Dance Festival when I met your dad. I had gone to the pub to celebrate with friends and the moment I walked in, I saw him. And he smiled, and that was that.'

'Has Dad seen you dance?'

'No. I told him I loved to dance when we first met, but he never had a chance to watch me . . . or maybe I never wanted him to.'

'Why not?' I ask, gently taking the photo from her grasp.

'I don't know.' She releases the picture, allowing me to hold it in my hand. It's warm from her touch, yet cold to me.

I want to ask her but I don't know how. I don't want to upset her more.

'Were you scared?' I finally ask.

She turns to me, and softly smiles. 'Maybe I was. Or maybe deep down I knew that part of my life was over.'

'Is that what you really wanted?'

'What do you mean?'

'Were you ready for it to be over?'

She pauses, pondering her response for a m[...] too long. As if she's lying, not wanting to tell [...] truth, not yet anyway.

'Yes.' She flattens the fabrics of her dress, smo[...] out the crinkles that I don't see. 'I was ready [...] new life.'

I have one last question. One last thing I w[...] know about her old life. One last thing I *need* to [...] 'Did seeing Olivia dance remind you of whe[...] danced?'

She smiles and looks ahead, as if she can sud[...] see Olivia dancing in front of her.

Leaping.

Bounding.

Infinitely floating.

'Of course. I loved to watch her. I wanted [...] succeed so badly. To do what I couldn't. She [...] her. She had the talent, the drive, the opport[...] wanted her to go to London so badly.' She p[...] hand on her mouth and seems to stifle a so[...] any way pushed her too much, I didn't mea[...]

'You didn't push her,' I say, gripping her [...] wanted her to be happy, and dancing an[...] London was what made her happy.'

She rests her hand on top of mine and s[...] down. Her hands are warm, familiar. The [...] fades and small creases form around her e[...]

Chapter Ten: 08.01.2016

The wind howls outside my window, thrashing against the glass. It pulls the branches in and out, and churns the leaves like a washing machine. It desperately wants in. I desperately want out.

I can't sleep. I keep trying but my thoughts weigh heavy in my mind, and I can't stop the nagging feeling of having left something behind. My dad used to say that a young mind shouldn't carry the burdens of an old mind. But maybe I'm not young any more. I don't feel young. I feel like I've lived more years in the past two weeks than anyone else on this island.

Is anyone sleeping out there?

Do they too worry about the killer still out there?

Is 'he' out there right now thinking that he got away with it?

Could 'he' be a 'she'?

'He' could be anyone, and that anyone could be waiting for me next.

I sit upright in my bed and throw the covers off my body. I'm cold, but I can't stand the heavy quilt on my skin. It itches. It burns. It's suffocating me.

I slide my legs out of the bed and down the frame until my feet touch the carpeted floor. Using my hand to steady myself on the wall, I fumble for the light switch on the lamp by the door and flip it on.

Nothing in my bedroom looks familiar any more. It all looks removed from who I am now. I don't remember why I picked out that wallpaper design, or why I chose to fill my bookshelves with framed dried flowers. The butterfly lamp, the lilac carpet, the handmade bunting above my bed, the half-filled water glasses that I accidentally left to evaporate and leave water rings on the wood beneath them. It all seems so trivial now. So meaningless.

I start by removing the bunting strung from the small metal hooks in the wall. I wrap it around my wrist then slide my arm out until a small pile remains in a snake-like shape. Then I slide the books off the shelves, one by one, each leaving a dust mark behind. No time to read. Besides, I don't need to read stories in a hard binding. My life is a story. One big plot, with twists and turns to keep the reader engaged, emotionally invested.

Then I take down the framed primroses, oyster plants, campions, yellows of coltsfoot and thistle. Next are the photos around my vanity mirror, stuck on with Blu-Tack and sticky tape. I delicately hold pictures of me with my friends and family in my palm. My fingers linger over a picture of Olivia and me.

I'm around three or four years old in the photo, and I have on a navy blue dress and I'm staring up at my sister with a big grin on my face. My eyes are stretched wide into thin slits, little lines on my temples and my teeth stick out, gums exposed. I'm laughing. My sister, tall and thin with a striped dress on, is bouncing on a pogo ball. She's in mid-air, her long dark hair in the air, her arms spread wide. And I'm just watching her, mesmerized. She was always my idol, my aspiration. I don't know if she ever knew that. As I got older, I just got too busy to tell her. But that never changed. That feeling of complete admiration.

I hold the photo to my chest and squeeze my eyes shut. Why didn't I tell her? How could I not tell her every day how much I loved and admired her? She always found the time to tell me.

I can't bear to let this photo go, so I place it gently in the top drawer of my bedside table and get back to the rest of the room. The colour. I can't stand the wallpaper colour. That's not even my favourite colour any more. Was it ever?

I start picking at a small section by the window with my nail, then I get a pen, and soon I'm down in the kitchen looking for Mum's cake slicer. Every time I tear a piece off, I feel relieved. I feel lighter, less burdened by the wind outside, by the killer inside my mind.

Soon I have most of the section around the window done, albeit a few chips into the plaster and siding. My fingers throb from the repetitive movement of pushing and pulling the cake slicer back and forth, back and forth.

I grab the fuzzy beige blanket from my chair and throw it on to the heap that's beginning to spill over from the centre of my bedroom floor. What next?

The little flower stickers on my drawers are so stupid. I'm not ten any more so why do I have them? I pick at them with my nails and manage to peel half of each off before they tear and rip in the middle, leaving a white residue on the drawer. I put those straight in the wastebasket.

I still see clutter everywhere. It's closing in on me.

I grab the floral box in the corner of my room that's sitting on a pile of *Seventeen* and *Glamour* magazines and slide it on the floor towards the bed. It feels heavy. I hoist it up over my bed covers onto the bed and sit with my legs crossed beside it.

The edges are covered in a thin layer of dust so I rub my hand over them and watch the particles fall onto the covers. I pop the cover up and slide it off. An old Kodak throwaway camera sits on the top. Underneath are some old papers – my essay on North Atlantic blackbird migration, a letter from my nana, even an old school progress report.

I read the first couple of lines: '. . . *bright . . . a day-dreamer . . . well-written essays . . . hard-working . . . punctual for school . . .*' Daydreamer was the only negative comment, and even that I didn't really think was negative. Everyone who lived on this island spent most of their time staring out the windows towards the mainland. Not me. I stared out of the window but not towards the

'You danced?'

She nods, her eyes never leaving the photo.

'You never told me that. Did Olivia know?'

'She found some old photos that Gran took of me at a ballet class. She kept one of them.'

'Oh, she never showed me,' I say, my voice exposing the disappointment. This was a piece of Mum that I never knew, a piece that my sister kept from me. Why would she do that?

'Olivia was already starting to show an interest in dance at that point, so I encouraged her. She reminded me so much of myself at that age. And she was good. Oh my god, she was good at it.'

'Yeah, she was.'

'She danced better than I ever could. She danced like she didn't care about anything. She was so brave in her dancing. I always felt like I held back.'

'What happened? Why did you stop?'

'I met your father.'

'How?'

'We met in the pub and that was that. I fell pregnant with Olivia shortly after and our families encouraged us to get married.'

'Oh.' Was this not the life Mum wanted? Had she not wanted to marry my dad?

'Don't get me wrong, I loved your father very much. Marrying him was the best thing I ever did. It gave me two beautiful daughters.' She wraps her arm around me and squeezes slightly.

'But you had to give up your dancing?'

'I thought after I had Olivia, I could get back into it but my body had changed. It just didn't respond the way it did before. It had given up on that life, and after a while, so did I.'

'What would have happened had you not met Dad?'

'I can't think like that, honey.'

'But if you had to, what would have happened?'

'Well, I had a place with a dance company in Edinburgh. We were about to train for the Edinburgh International Dance Festival when I met your dad. I had gone to the pub to celebrate with friends and the moment I walked in, I saw him. And he smiled, and that was that.'

'Has Dad seen you dance?'

'No. I told him I loved to dance when we first met, but he never had a chance to watch me . . . or maybe I never wanted him to.'

'Why not?' I ask, gently taking the photo from her grasp.

'I don't know.' She releases the picture, allowing me to hold it in my hand. It's warm from her touch, yet cold to me.

I want to ask her but I don't know how. I don't want to upset her more.

'Were you scared?' I finally ask.

She turns to me, and softly smiles. 'Maybe I was. Or maybe deep down I knew that part of my life was over.'

'Is that what you really wanted?'

'What do you mean?'

'Were you ready for it to be over?'

She pauses, pondering her response for a moment too long. As if she's lying, not wanting to tell me the truth, not yet anyway.

'Yes.' She flattens the fabrics of her dress, smoothing out the crinkles that I don't see. 'I was ready for my new life.'

I have one last question. One last thing I want to know about her old life. One last thing I *need* to know. 'Did seeing Olivia dance remind you of when you danced?'

She smiles and looks ahead, as if she can suddenly see Olivia dancing in front of her.

Leaping.

Bounding.

Infinitely floating.

'Of course. I loved to watch her. I wanted her to succeed so badly. To do what I couldn't. She had it in her. She had the talent, the drive, the opportunities. I wanted her to go to London so badly.' She places her hand on her mouth and seems to stifle a sob. 'If I in any way pushed her too much, I didn't mean to. I –'

'You didn't push her,' I say, gripping her hand. 'You wanted her to be happy, and dancing and going to London was what made her happy.'

She rests her hand on top of mine and softly presses down. Her hands are warm, familiar. Then her smile fades and small creases form around her eyes. She gets up, straightens her dress and looks around as if she can't remember what she came in here for.

'I should start dinner. Your dad will be home soon. Please don't touch anything in here.'

And just like that, the small window that opened up for me to climb through closes.

I return to my own bedroom after she leaves, and close the door behind me.

Her words linger in my mind, and I close my eyes to stop the tears from falling. I collapse on my bed and pull the covers in towards my chin. It's too early to sleep, too dark to face the day.

My dad lost his best friend that night. My mum lost a piece of her that night. I know what I lost. But what is left behind? What do I have to offer my mum and dad? I'm not her.

The wrong person died that night.

And everyone is thinking that.

Chapter Ten: 08.01.2016

The wind howls outside my window, thrashing against the glass. It pulls the branches in and out, and churns the leaves like a washing machine. It desperately wants in. I desperately want out.

I can't sleep. I keep trying but my thoughts weigh heavy in my mind, and I can't stop the nagging feeling of having left something behind. My dad used to say that a young mind shouldn't carry the burdens of an old mind. But maybe I'm not young any more. I don't feel young. I feel like I've lived more years in the past two weeks than anyone else on this island.

Is anyone sleeping out there?

Do they too worry about the killer still out there?

Is 'he' out there right now thinking that he got away with it?

Could 'he' be a 'she'?

'He' could be anyone, and that anyone could be waiting for me next.

I sit upright in my bed and throw the covers off my body. I'm cold, but I can't stand the heavy quilt on my skin. It itches. It burns. It's suffocating me.

I slide my legs out of the bed and down the frame until my feet touch the carpeted floor. Using my hand to steady myself on the wall, I fumble for the light switch on the lamp by the door and flip it on.

Nothing in my bedroom looks familiar any more. It all looks removed from who I am now. I don't remember why I picked out that wallpaper design, or why I chose to fill my bookshelves with framed dried flowers. The butterfly lamp, the lilac carpet, the handmade bunting above my bed, the half-filled water glasses that I accidentally left to evaporate and leave water rings on the wood beneath them. It all seems so trivial now. So meaningless.

I start by removing the bunting strung from the small metal hooks in the wall. I wrap it around my wrist then slide my arm out until a small pile remains in a snake-like shape. Then I slide the books off the shelves, one by one, each leaving a dust mark behind. No time to read. Besides, I don't need to read stories in a hard binding. My life is a story. One big plot, with twists and turns to keep the reader engaged, emotionally invested.

Then I take down the framed primroses, oyster plants, campions, yellows of coltsfoot and thistle. Next are the photos around my vanity mirror, stuck on with Blu-Tack and sticky tape. I delicately hold pictures of me with my friends and family in my palm. My fingers linger over a picture of Olivia and me.

I'm around three or four years old in the photo, and I have on a navy blue dress and I'm staring up at my sister with a big grin on my face. My eyes are stretched wide into thin slits, little lines on my temples and my teeth stick out, gums exposed. I'm laughing. My sister, tall and thin with a striped dress on, is bouncing on a pogo ball. She's in mid-air, her long dark hair in the air, her arms spread wide. And I'm just watching her, mesmerized. She was always my idol, my aspiration. I don't know if she ever knew that. As I got older, I just got too busy to tell her. But that never changed. That feeling of complete admiration.

I hold the photo to my chest and squeeze my eyes shut. Why didn't I tell her? How could I not tell her every day how much I loved and admired her? She always found the time to tell me.

I can't bear to let this photo go, so I place it gently in the top drawer of my bedside table and get back to the rest of the room. The colour. I can't stand the wallpaper colour. That's not even my favourite colour any more. Was it ever?

I start picking at a small section by the window with my nail, then I get a pen, and soon I'm down in the kitchen looking for Mum's cake slicer. Every time I tear a piece off, I feel relieved. I feel lighter, less burdened by the wind outside, by the killer inside my mind.

Soon I have most of the section around the window done, albeit a few chips into the plaster and siding. My fingers throb from the repetitive movement of pushing and pulling the cake slicer back and forth, back and forth.

I grab the fuzzy beige blanket from my chair and throw it on to the heap that's beginning to spill over from the centre of my bedroom floor. What next?

The little flower stickers on my drawers are so stupid. I'm not ten any more so why do I have them? I pick at them with my nails and manage to peel half of each off before they tear and rip in the middle, leaving a white residue on the drawer. I put those straight in the wastebasket.

I still see clutter everywhere. It's closing in on me.

I grab the floral box in the corner of my room that's sitting on a pile of *Seventeen* and *Glamour* magazines and slide it on the floor towards the bed. It feels heavy. I hoist it up over my bed covers onto the bed and sit with my legs crossed beside it.

The edges are covered in a thin layer of dust so I rub my hand over them and watch the particles fall onto the covers. I pop the cover up and slide it off. An old Kodak throwaway camera sits on the top. Underneath are some old papers – my essay on North Atlantic blackbird migration, a letter from my nana, even an old school progress report.

I read the first couple of lines: '. . . *bright . . . a day-dreamer . . . well-written essays . . . hard-working . . . punctual for school* . . .' Daydreamer was the only negative comment, and even that I didn't really think was negative. Everyone who lived on this island spent most of their time staring out the windows towards the mainland. Not me. I stared out of the window but not towards the mainland. I looked deeper into Orkney, towards the hills, the stones, the small thatched cottages and wood-burning fireplaces. While everyone, especially Olivia, looked south towards Aberdeen, Glasgow, Edinburgh, even London, I looked north towards Rousay and Westray. This was always enough for me.

I lift the papers up and find more photos. Gathering up as much as my hands can manage I spill them out onto my bed covers and start prodding through them with my fingers.

I find one with my dad. He's young, maybe in his early or mid thirties, and he's wearing beige cords and a white T-shirt with red and blue stripes. His dark hair is bushy and a little wild, and he has aviator-style sunglasses on. He's sitting on a skateboard and my sister and I are behind him trying to push him on it. He's laughing, Olivia's laughing, but I'm focusing hard, my face strained, my hands tight on his back.

My dad used to say I was always just a little bit too serious for life. He calls me 'delicate'. Maybe I was delicate. Because now I feel broken, shattered into a thousand pieces that not even the strongest glue can patch together.

I hold up a picture of my sister dancing. She's reaching her arms out in front of her, off to an angle, while her back leg is up and out. She told me what this was once. Now I try to remember.

Arabesque.

That's it. *Arabesque.*

She's wearing a black leotard and grey shorts. She's trying not to smile, but I can tell she wants to. Her eyes are shimmering and her jaw is tensed, the corners of her mouth slightly turning up.

There's more of her dancing. Dozens more. She's jumping in the air during a concert or a performance of some sort. In another, she's young, maybe six or seven, and she's standing at a ballet barre and has her feet rotated out. *From the hips*, she'd always tell me when I would pretend to be her.

And I always did.

I would dance around the room like her, while she clapped and laughed with me. My mum always said I had 'two left feet', whatever that means. I never had her elegance, her beauty. I was always . . . just me.

I suddenly shiver, feeling a cool breeze wash over me. My eyes are pulled towards the window. When did it get light out? My clock reads 08.28. I look down at my hands, still red and achy from slicing the wallpaper so hard. A little cut on my thumb stings from where I went over it with the cake slicer. I squeeze my index finger to my thumb and push down, until a little bubble of blood sits on the surface. Then I wipe it with my other hand and watch the bright red blood smear between my fingers. I remember the blood around my sister's hairline when I saw her.

Why aren't people telling me anything? Do they forget I'm here, that I'm waiting?

I stand up and march over to my wardrobe. I pull

out blue skinny jeans, woollen ribbed socks, my hiking boots, and throw a thick Fair Isle jumper over my pyjama top. I rush down the stairs to my thick navy coat with the fur around the hood, and slip it on, fastening all the toggles. I feel the house key in my left pocket, and a £5 note for the bus in my right. I slip out the back door, being careful not to let it slam shut in the wind, and hurry down the stone path and out the gate that Dad never got around to fixing.

The air is bitter cold and the bright sun hurts my eyes a little. It must have snowed last night because the tips of the grass are frosty white and the ground crunches under my boots.

I look over to the left of the road and see sheep already out, searching for soft grass to graze on under the sun. The ice should melt soon. Snow never sits too long on the ground, not any more. Climate change. That's what my geography teacher says.

A car passes me – red, old paintwork and a rectangular shape to the body. Then another – silver, looks like Siobhan's dad's Honda Accord.

I step up on the grassy embankment when I round the corner in case the cars don't see me, and feel the ground slipping under the soles of my shoes. I steady myself by placing a hand on the pole of the wired fencing, and find my footing back on the road. I see the bus stop. There are already two people waiting for the next bus.

By the time the bus arrives, the £5 note is warm and

crumpled in my palm. I straighten it out as much as possible and hand it to the driver. My house disappears behind me as the bus pulls me further and further from the box of photos and memories in my bedroom.

The bus stops next to the Red Cross shop where Siobhan's mum works. I quickly cross the street before she sees me through the window and tries to talk to me. The police station sits on a bend in the street, not too far of a walk from where my sister's body was found. I think on an average day, the walk could take someone up to thirty minutes, but that day it took me half that time. I don't remember running but I remember moving fast, very fast. Maybe I was running. I don't seem to remember much from that day now. It's all a blur.

When I arrive, the receptionist is gone from her desk so I have to wait. When she returns she has a steaming cup of tea in one hand and a digestive biscuit in the other.

'Oh, it's you again . . . um, do your mum and dad know you're here?'

'Yes,' I lie. 'Is DI Birkens in yet?'

She puts her mug down on her planner and I see a drop slide down the ceramic onto her planner underneath. I refrain from telling her.

'No, he's not in yet.'

'OK, I'll wait,' I say, sitting down in one of the chairs. Perhaps the magazines will have been updated. I've already read most of them.

'He won't like you sitting here, not when he comes in,' she tells me, before taking a big bite of her biscuit.

I stand up, 'OK, then I'll wait across the street. Can you tell him to meet me in the hotel restaurant down the road past the Standing Stones?'

She stops chewing, seeming to ponder over my request, then eventually nods and gets back to dunking the rest of her digestive into her tea.

When I sit down in the restaurant, I order a mug of tea with milk and two sugars, and some biscuits, digestives if they have. They don't. But they give me three Hob Nobs.

The hotel is still decorated for Christmas. Garlands loop around the archway of the main entrance, and a big fake tree sits in the corner of the restaurant, glittered with big red and gold balls, and a sparkly silver star on top. The tip of the tree sags slightly to the left under the weight of the big star, lightly touching the pale pink wall beside it.

I'm there for less than ten minutes when Birkens walks in through the door. A little bell jingles when the door opens and a gust of cold air pushes in from the outside.

He spots me almost immediately and starts to walk over. He stops and asks the waitress behind the bar for something. A strong coffee, I think.

He sits down in front of me, taking the chair closest to the window. He doesn't say anything, not even a Hi. He just turns his head and looks out of the window at the road outside. 'How are you getting on with your new FLO?'

'My new what?'

'Your Family Liaison Officer.'

'Oh, her.'

'Yes, her. She's there to support you, did you know that?'

'She doesn't do much. She just makes cups of tea all the time.'

Birkens scoffs, then straightens his expression. 'Go easy on her, it's her first case.'

I stir my tea again, the metal clinking against the china. 'Is this Allans' first case too?'

'Dave is experienced within the police force, and is a valuable member of the team. Besides, he'll be a detective constable soon.'

My spoon clinks against the side as I gaze up at him. The corners of his mouth turn up slightly, exposing a faint smirk.

'OK, yes. It's his first homicide case.'

'Quite a team they gave you,' I say sarcastically, taking a big gulp of hot tea. It burns my tongue slightly and the roof of my mouth, but I take another sip. 'But this isn't your first case?'

He looks out the window, beyond the paved streets and occasional cyclist. 'No, sadly, I've had quite a few cases over the years.'

'And how have they ended? Did you solve every one?'

He squirms slightly in his chair. The waitress arrives

with his coffee, and he suddenly sits up straight, seeming glad of her timing.

'Here you go. Milk?' she asks him. Her top teeth are lightly stained with her coral lipstick.

He shakes his head No, half smiling, half not. Then turns back to me.

'So, when was the last time you saw your sister with James?' he asks.

'Um, I'm not really sure,' I answer, a little too quickly. I'm supposed to be the one asking him questions.

'Take your time.'

I pause and look out of the window. I remember snow falling, and dark setting in early, really early. That's right, it was the shortest day of the year. 'I think it was at the Winter Solstice feast. James and Emily came to meet her at the house and they walked down there together.'

'And where was that?'

'Maeshowe.'

He nods. 'Of course.'

'You've never been?'

He shakes his head and takes another sip of his coffee, slurping at the end.

'How could you live in Orkney and never go to one?'

'I haven't been here for that long, remember? Plus, I don't tend to . . . *mingle* with a lot of people.'

'Do you prefer being alone?'

'Sort of, yes.'

'Me too now, I think.'

He sighs, and stares at me for a beat too long. I awkwardly brush my hair behind my ears and look out at the sheep dotted on the muddy hills. Snow never really does stick on the hills any more. I had to write an essay once for my geography class about climate changes in high latitude places, like Orkney. It was interesting, and sad at the same time. It made me want to write a letter to our local MP to campaign for saving trees. Deforestation causes an increase in carbon dioxide in the air. No one ever wrote back. So I hid my mum's hairspray. It was all I could think of at the time. I doubt that did anything. Anyway, she just bought another can.

'What are you thinking about?'

'Nothing really.'

I hold the mug of tea in both my palms and feel the warmth penetrate my skin.

'Do you know how old Maeshowe is?'

I shrug my shoulders up and wait for him to tell me. I like the sound of his voice right now. It's soothing. And it makes me forget his voice from the day we found Olivia's body. That voice sounded sad, tired, and maybe even a little angry.

'They think it was built 2,800 years before the common era.'

'What does that mean?'

'It means before Christ.'

'Why don't they just say that then? We learnt about BC and AD in RE.'

'Well, that's not the term they use now I hear. We're supposed to say BCE – Before the Common Era.'

'Why?'

'Because BC and AD are Christian terms.'

'Do you not go to church?'

He squirms uncomfortably in his chair like a thousand ants are crawling up his legs. 'Um . . . I used to.'

'Why did you stop?'

He puts his mug down on the table in front of him and clasps his hands together. He doesn't look like he's going to respond to that question so I ask him another one.

'Who's they?'

'Hmm?'

'You said "they" don't use BC and AD any more?'

'Oh right, I mean archeologists.'

'I thought archeologists only dug up dinosaur bones,' I smile. It feels funny on my face so I stop.

He laughs. 'No, no, they do a lot more than that.'

'Are you interested in archeology?'

'I read a little historical non-fiction every now and then. Your mum says you like to read. What do you read?'

'Sometimes I read books about flowers.'

'Flowers?'

'It's silly, really. But sometimes I find a flower and I dry it and frame it.'

'Why?'

'I don't know. Maybe I think I'll never find it again. Maybe I want to capture it before I lose it.'

His eyebrows furrow and for a moment he looks like he's in pain. I wonder what he's thinking about. He grips his mug tighter. Maybe I should talk about something else. 'Did you read any books about Maeshowe?'

He glances up and his face begins to soften slightly. 'Actually, yes.'

'Is it true that there are dead bodies under it?'

'Well, you know, they say the cairn was built as a monument to the dead. That for three weeks before and after the winter solstice, the rays from the sun shine through the passageway into the chamber to signify that loved ones who have passed away are resting in peace in another life.'

Did my sister believe that? Over a week has passed now. Did I miss her light? Did she try and reach out to me during this time?

'Of course that's all stories now. But people enjoy hearing them. You know, Mhairi at the front desk says she once got a call from a neighbour down the street from Maeshowe who saw a man carrying a large wooden cross almost the size of him all the way up to the cairn. Another year, police had to escort about twenty to thirty people from a private jet to the ruins who had flown all the way from America because they wanted to lay crystals on the site.'

'Really? Were they real crystals?'

'Who knows,' he laughs. He checks his watch. 'How

did your sister act that night as she was leaving for the solstice feast?'

'She seemed herself, I guess.'

'So nothing out of the ordinary?'

'No.'

'And how was James?'

'He was fine too.'

'Did you talk to him?'

'I always talk to him. They'd been together for almost four years. I would never have guessed they had already broken up, although they didn't hug or anything when he came in the house. They always used to before.'

'They broke up?'

'Yeah, that's what James said when I went by his house.'

'And when was that?'

'I think a day or two after Olivia was reported missing. I went there looking for her, and to Emily's. I thought maybe Olivia had drunk too much and was too embarrassed to come home.'

'Did she usually drink too much?'

'No I didn't mean that. I mean . . . she drank of course. Everyone drinks here. There's not much else to do.'

'Right. Do you?'

'Sometimes, but not a lot'

'Why not?'

'I don't like the taste. It tastes like petrol.'

'Yeah, I guess it does,' he smiles. 'So did James say anything else about why they broke up?'

'No, just that they broke up and he didn't know where she was and didn't care.'

'He said that, that he didn't care?'

'I don't remember. I may have assumed he meant that. I don't know.'

He glances at his watch again, and slides his chair back.

'Do you have to leave?' I ask.

'I'm afraid so, I have some new information I need to check out.'

'Anything you can tell me?'

He smiles, and heads for the door. 'Thanks for our chat, Alexandra.'

'It's Alex!' I call after him.

'I know,' he says, as he walks under the garland-decorated archway and disappears around the corner.

Chapter Eleven: 10.01.2016

My dreams are all of her.

My thoughts are consumed by her.

I can see her.

I can hear her.

I can even smell the perfume she wears sometimes. Rose, cinnamon and sandalwood.

She's playing hide-and-seek in my dream tonight. I'm walking through our house, but it's not really our house. I just think it is in this dream. I count loudly, as my feet barely touch the wooden floor. I'm not supposed to be walking and counting, I know that. I'm cheating. But Olivia always let me cheat if it meant that I would win the game. She always wanted me to win. Even if she'd placed a small wager on the game – a piece of chewing gum, a pound coin, a chocolate penny from her Christmas stocking. I'd win. And she'd pay.

When I reach the number ten, my steps get louder. My feet land on the wood a little harder so she knows I've stopped counting and I'm now searching. First, I look in her bedroom. I walk in and see the wall covered in photos of her and her friends, in the shape of an O. I hold up her quilt and look under the bed. Nothing. Then I open her mahogany wardrobe. Empty. I glance under her desk, where her postcards from different countries around the world sit, then close the door behind me.

Next, I go into my parents' bedroom. Their room is colder than mine. Dad likes to sleep with the window slightly ajar, even though Mum is always cold. The bed frame goes all the way down to the ground, with the underside converted into storage drawers to hold our bed linens and towels, so I know she's not under there.

My fingertips graze the tops of the drawers, occasionally catching on the metal spiral frames holding photos of us as children. Olivia's school photo – pigtails, goofy smile. My school photo – French braid that's so tight it's making my eyes water slightly in the photo, and a thick scratchy jumper my mum made me on her knitting machine that has a big yellow parrot on the chest. I was bullied for days about that jumper. Olivia told me just to wear it more to shut them up. I always did what she told me to do.

There's a photo of my mum and dad on their wedding day outside St John's church. And last, one of mum's parents. I never really got to meet them. My gran died when I was really small, and my granddad passed away when I was around six or seven. But I remember his thick Irish brogue, the grey and red jumpers that my mum knitted for him, and his smile. I faintly remember his smile.

He used to give me pennies from a tall glass jar to

go to the shop with Olivia to get myself a magazine and sometimes if I was really lucky, a sweet too. I also remember how close my mum was to her father. Even if I don't remember him, I can clearly recall their unconditional love for each other.

They talked a lot about her mother. They missed her so much, and they connected through their shared sorrow. I wish I'd known my grandparents better. I wish they'd lived longer so I could have remembered them more. They could have been here for us, for my mum. They could have helped us through this, if a way forward even exists.

But I wish a lot of things right now.

I move past the frames and place my hands on the doorknobs of their walk-in wardrobe. I find shoeboxes, stacks of magazines, plastic bags of wool, but not my sister.

Now I don't hear her.

I don't see her.

And I don't smell her perfume any more.

My hands grab at door handles, my eyes skim under tables, beds, and behind doors. I get tired of the game, and start calling her name.

Olivia!

Olivia!

But she doesn't answer. She doesn't call out to me to expose her location and end the game. She must know I want to end it. I'm crying now. The tears are cold in my dream, not warm, and they don't spill down my cheeks. Instead they curl and coil around my arm like the blood in my last dream.

My dream ends when I'm still looking for her, so abrupt and so real.

When I wake, a bright light hurts my eye so I close them tight again. When I blink them open, I notice that I've slept later than I wanted. So why do I feel so tired still?

I know it's a dream, but I still feel like I'm in the middle of a game with her. It feels unfinished. Like she's waiting for me to find her still. But I've given up. Moved on. Got tired of the game.

A sharp knock on the door tells me it's time to start getting dressed for the funeral.

The funeral.

We have been begging DI Birkens for days to let us bury Olivia, but now the day is here, I want it to go away again. I'm not ready to bury my sister. I'm not ready to say goodbye.

I roll over into my pillow and feel the tears come. I bite down on the fabric to stop myself from screaming. I can't breathe, but I don't lift my head. I don't want to let the cold air – the reality – in. I cry harder into the pillow, feeling my upper back ache. Then I stop.

It's the funeral today so I have to be strong. I have to greet people, thank them for coming, stand by my parents. I can't cry. There's no time for crying.

After I shower, I slip into the only black dress I own but I don't have black shoes. Maybe Olivia will.

When I push her bedroom door open, the first thing I see is the big photo montage O. Then I see her trainers on the bedroom floor, a book she's been reading on her nightstand, an old coffee mug. I see her everywhere, but it's only remnants of her. It's not really Olivia.

The police have been in here. I can tell. Some things are missing, moved. I had wanted it to stay the same. But nothing stays the same. Everything changes. Everyone dies.

My fingers graze the doorway. It's marked up in different pens, markers. Even a purple paint splotch. She loved to measure himself. She loved to see herself growing up. She wanted to grow up so badly. And now she never will.

My thumb strokes the last marking – 5 feet 6 and a half inches. It's written in red pen. That was her last height, before she died.

I sink to my knees and touch the first marking, when she was just three years old. It's my dad's writing. I see one I did. I spelled inches wrong. I must have only been about seven or eight. That's my one. I did that with her. I didn't do any more after that.

I touch my forehead to the doorframe and try to remember her. I can see her. She's standing against the frame with her back against it. Her long hair curls down her back and she looks at me, smiling. She drags the chair over from her desk and holds my hand as I stand up on it. Then she hurries back to the frame, and hands me a blue marker. Her chin tips upwards slightly so the crown of her head touches the wood.

I lean over, placing a hand on her shoulder to steady myself and draw a horizontal line across where her head sits. She giggles and asks me, 'Have I grown?'

I can't remember any more. I won't. It hurts too much.

I move inside and close the door behind me. My body slides down, slowly, an inch at a time, like on the frame, until I hit the floor. I can feel my face contort until it hurts, the tears spilling out. They drop onto the ground around me.

I hear the floor creak outside the bedroom door, and deep breathing from behind it. 'Alex?'

I rub the tears away with the back of my hand, and take a deep breath. I need to be strong for my parents. 'Yeah, it's me.' I wait for her, but she won't come in. She can't come in, it's too hard for her.

'What are you doing in there?'

'Just looking for shoes. Do you know where Olivia . . .' It hurts to say her name out loud to my mum. And I know it hurts her. I clear my throat and try again. 'Do you know where Olivia put her black shoes?'

My mum doesn't say anything.

Please don't make me say it again.

'No,' she says softly.

'OK.'

'Alex?'

'Yeah.'

'Can you pick out an outfit for today?'

'I'm already dressed.'

I hear a croaking noise, like she's muffling a cry. 'Mum?'

'No, I mean an outfit for your sister. We need to drop it off at the funeral home this morning before we get to the church to help set up.'

Oh. An outfit for my sister to be buried in. Her last outfit. The last thing she'll ever wear before the earth is put down on top of her. Why do *I* have to do this?

'I'm sorry,' my mum whimpers from behind the door.

I need to be strong.

I need to be strong.

I clear my throat sharply and take a deep breath. 'No, that's fine. I'll look something out.'

She's still waiting at the door, waiting for something. But I can't hear any more about it, or say any more about it. 'I'll be down in ten, Mum.'

'Thank you.' The stairs creak under her feet. She's gone.

Olivia's bedroom seems so much smaller now. Like the walls are closing in. I go to her closet and reach out my hand. My fingers tremble as I pull roughly on the handle. Purple coat hangers swing gently on the metal rod, and layers of fabrics, all different colours, hang just inches from my face.

A string of fabric daisies hang on a small metal hook inside the door and dangle down to the base of the cupboard. They would look pretty inside her coffin with her, maybe laid around her head. I think she would like that.

It will be hard to pick out just one thing for her to wear. My sister looked so pretty in everything she wore. She had a red dress with a gold clip on the shoulder that she had worn for Christmas lunch one year. She loved to dress up for the day. We all did. We'd sit around in our pyjamas all morning opening presents and sipping coffee. Then we'd go upstairs to get dressed into our Christmas day outfits, which were clothes we'd never wear at any other time of year. Even I would wear a dress – something my sister would pick out, of course. And we'd come down and take pictures by the tree, and eat until our bellies were about to explode. Then we'd snuggle up on the sofa together and watch telly while we argued over who'd eaten all the purple Quality Streets.

She could wear that today.

No. That dress is special. I don't want to bury it too.

She has a black dress that had little sparkly cotton pieces throughout it. She'd bought it at Topshop for Emily's birthday night out last year.

No. She shouldn't wear black to her own funeral. Even she'd say that.

Then there's the blue dress. Royal blue. With the capped sleeves and the frilly skirt. She'd bought that at River Island after she decided to move to London. She called it her first London Dress. The tags are still on it. She hadn't even had the chance to wear it yet. And now she never would.

So I choose the blue, so she could wear it for the first and last time. And because she loved to lie on the grass in the garden and gaze up at the birds soaring high above. Blue said that. The blue said many things, although no dress or top would ever truly represent Olivia. She was special and I couldn't replicate that with a good dress and a coffin decorated with plastic daisies.

I close the cupboard, take one last glance at her bedroom and how she left it – how the police had tried to leave it – then exit the space as if I was never there. As if my feet hadn't touched the carpet on her floor, as if my fingers hadn't grazed the clothes on the hangers, and as if my tears hadn't dropped onto the fabric between my hands.

Chapter Twelve: 10.01.2016

I rest my head against the window and watch the houses pass by, one after another, each draped in a thick sheet of fog. It's everywhere today. It gathers at the edge of the ocean, hangs over the river, and slithers up and down the streets of Stromness. It makes the world outside so quiet, blanketing sounds and blurring shapes. It reminds me of my dreams.

The car hits a crack in the road and dips slightly, pushing my forehead away from the glass. I didn't want to ride with my sister's body to the church this afternoon. I couldn't. Siobhan's mum offered to take me, and my dad was too tired to argue so he said yes. I could see the disappointment in my mum's eyes as I left. She had wanted us to all drive there together. One big happy family. Her, me, my dad, and my dead sister. All in one car, as if nothing's changed and we're just on our way to church on a Sunday morning.

But we're not. And everything has changed.

I see my sister in the casket, dressed in royal blue with daisies strewn around her head, and I remember why I didn't want to get in the car with my parents.

When we turn into Graham Place and see the steeple peek out from the shop buildings and commercial rooftops, the fog pulls back as if it's allowing us to enter. It waits at the stairs for us to park, get out, and ascend. It follows us to the front door, and then retreats up the red stone walls.

A small crowd gathers outside, waiting for the immediate family to enter first. My parents are already there. My dad wraps his arm around my shoulders while my mum weakly feigns gratitude and thanks people for coming.

Black crows circle above us, and squawk over the rooftops. One drifts away from the flock, and lands on the iron cross above my head, near the steeple. Its head is dipped low as if it's watching me, waiting for something.

My dad squeezes my arm and I feel my body being ushered through the doorway. Inside, large bouquets of white carnations adorn the pews, aisles and credence table. On the table sits a large gold goblet, and a small circular plate filled with the holy bread.

A smile creeps over my face as I think about how few times we came here when Olivia was alive.

Clusters of people shuffle in behind us, each selecting a pew and quickly sitting down. I didn't know there were so many variations on a black dress. Some have ruffled sleeves, others have no sleeves at all, a few even have a little sparkle woven into the fabric, while a couple are a little shorter above the knee than I would have expected for a funeral service.

I look forward, my feet not feeling like they're fully secure on the ground beneath me. My sister lies up ahead, her face aimed towards the ceiling of the church, towards the sky beyond it. My dad drops his hands, and releases me. Now my feet aren't moving at all, but he's drifting further and further away from me like the crow from its flock.

My mum is sitting down already, in the first pew. Her hand covers her mouth, as if she wants to scream loudly. My dad stops at the casket, and I hear whispers behind me. I turn back and see a sea of faces looking at me, looking at my mother, at my father. No one is looking at my sister.

Some I recognize, many from school, while others are new to me, unfamiliar. When I catch their eye, they either smile nervously or they quickly look away.

Our family liaison officer is here. She smiles at me and nods her head and sits in the way back. She looks nice today. She's wearing a black trouser suit, with a small white flower in the chest pocket. Her hair is pulled back in a nice way too.

I don't know her that well but I want to sit beside her for some reason. I want to sit in the way back. I want to be a spectator, an observer, not a participant in this funeral.

When my eyes drift out again, I see Andy. He's sitting beside Siobhan and her mum. He waves when I find him, but I don't wave back. When I look back out front, my dad is still standing there.

Father Raymond walks to him, his robe swaying gently. He delicately places a hand on my dad's arm. My dad startles and then moves to the pew to sit next to Mum.

I know everyone is ready to begin, ready to start so it can end. But I'm not ready.

I'm not ready.

Music trickles out from the speakers around me, turned low but still audible. I've heard this song before. It played in my sister's bedroom not too long ago. She stretched out on her bedroom floor listening to the strings, piano and fragile chorus, as she painted her toe nails. I can even remember the colour. Rose. But not a bold rose, a gentle rose, like one that's still touched by morning dew, slightly drowning out the hue.

For everyone else here, this song doesn't mean that. For them, this song is just a song. It's just a piece of music that's been picked to help set a particular tone, to help remind people of the person we lost. But for me, this song is so much more.

This song is *her*.

My chest heaves in and out, my breath shallow and loud. My fingers flicker uncontrollably beside my thighs.

The whispering gets louder behind me. They're talking about me. But I don't care. I don't care about anything any more.

When I look back, I see DI Birkens finally. Perhaps

I had been waiting for him. We couldn't start, not without him.

He's standing at the back, at the edge of one of the benches. His long dark coat flows past his hips and ends a little below his knees. He's wearing a white shirt and a black tie, and he even looks like he shaved this morning. His eyes are dark, and his face is tight like he's tensing. He doesn't want to be here either. He's not looking at Allans, who's already seated on the bench. He's not looking at my parents who hold each other. He's not looking at the casket which holds my sister, the most important person to me in the world.

He's looking at me.

He nods his head, and I nod back, not knowing what it means. Then he glances over at the pew where my parents sit and I know it's time for me to go to them. It's time for us to begin the goodbyes.

When I sit, my mum squeezes my hand and I feel her wedding band dig into my skin slightly. It's thick and silver, with a small flower design etched on the front, and the date of their wedding on the inside. She never takes it off, even in the shower. She wears it every minute of every day, because it represents something. Not the life she left behind for this family, but the life she created with us.

Father Raymond talks, he speaks the liturgies of the word and the Eucharist. He recites passages from the New Testament. And then it's my mum's turn to talk.

My dad chose to speak at the reception after. I asked to not say anything.

My mum recalls a story from when Olivia was nine or ten and she first asked about heaven. It was just after my granddad had died, and we both had questions about where a person goes after they leave the earth. My mum said she had told her that heaven is a place that we all visit, but that it looks different to each of us. For Olivia, it was a wide-open stage where she could dance and be free.

I know for me it would be a vast field filled with rare flowers and soft grass, still damp from the early morning dew. When I look back, I see Birkens has his head down and I wonder what he's thinking about. I wonder what his version of heaven would look like. I wonder if it would be a place, or simply a person. Who is this person that he hides so well?

When I look back, my mum has already left the stand. She's back beside me. It's Emily's turn, but she's not there. She's at the side of the pews, being comforted by her mum. Her cries are loud, her pain reverberating around the church walls. She can't walk, she can't speak. I want to go to her and tell her that it's OK. She doesn't have to speak if she can't. Everyone will understand. I chose not to speak.

But before I can stand, James is up out of his seat. He's walking to the front and raising the microphone slightly to his lips. He smiles at Emily, and opens his mouth. His words are gentle, pure. They talk of his love for my sister, and his love for my family. He apologizes to us. He apologizes to everyone. He feels guilty. We all do. He ends his speech with a short verse from Sir Walter Scott, chosen because he had once climbed the Scott Monument in Edinburgh and taken a photo from the top for my sister. He'd printed a copy and given it to her, with a message on the back about how they would visit the monument together one day, on their way to London.

> Look not thou on beauty's charming,
> Sit thou still when kings are arming,
> Taste not when the wine-cup glistens,
> Speak not when the people listens,
> Stop thine ear against the singer,
> From the red gold keep thy finger;
> Vacant heart and hand and eye,
> Easy live and quiet die.

He had wanted to go with her to London, been willing to leave this island and his family for her. He had loved her so much. What had happened between them? Why did Olivia end it?

The music ends, and Father Raymond talks again. When I turn around, people are shuffling back out the door they came in. Swathes of black sway side to side, and disappear from the church.

Then it's empty.

We slide off the pew, each taking a moment with

Olivia before we slip out the door into the stark winter sun.

Crowds gather again at the door, each with out-stretched hands, wanting to touch us, take our hand. Birkens stands with the family liaison officer talking, but it looks like Allans has already left. I didn't expect the police to stay for the wake.

My feet step further away from the church doors, further into the sunlight. Then I stop. I turn back, needing one last look before the casket is closed for ever, and no one will ever look upon her face again. My shoes slap against the marble aisle as I hurry back up. Knees trembling, I get closer and grip the edge of the casket to steady myself. A flicker of red draws my eye and I reach my hand in towards her body. My fingers accidentally graze her arm, and a small scream escapes my lips. She's cold, so cold. And hard. Not the soft, warm Olivia that I remember. No, this is something entirely different. A body. An empty, cold, hard body.

I look down and see a single red rose in my hand. A red rose in a sea of crisp white carnations.

'What is that?'

I turn and see Birkens standing at the foot of the steps, pointing towards the rose.

'I don't know. It's not mine. I just found it in her casket.'

'Was it there during the funeral?'

'No, it wasn't. Do you think someone put it here?'

Birkens nods and looks around, the church completely

empty, void of warmth and colour. The red rose looks strange here, out of place.

'Did *he* put it here?' I ask, the rose shaking slightly in my palm.

'I don't know. But I need to take it, if you don't mind.' He reaches out and takes it from me, wrapping it in a large white handkerchief.

I look back at my sister, my last moment with her tainted by a single red rose, and then follow Birkens out of the church.

Chapter Thirteen: 11.01.2016

The reception after the funeral had a good turnout as I knew it would: my sister was very popular. Everyone loved the blue dress I chose – her favourite colour was blue. She once bought the exact same cardigan in three different shades of blue, she always did stuff like that and I would always laugh at her.

I close my eyes and remember those times – I ache for her company, her laughter.

At the reception, people brought flowers and hugged the family, but again I felt invisible. I felt so disconnected from what was happening around me the entire time. I didn't hear a word Father Raymond said to me, or even my father's speech after the whisky was passed out. People were moving around me in a blur while I just sat there and stared at the crowds snaking around the pillars of the pub, fighting over the trays of sandwiches and platters of sausage rolls. I didn't even hear Andy calling my name until he touched me on the arm. When he did, I startled and looked at him like I had never seen him before.

He looked different to me. Everyone looked strange to me at the reception, like they were all playing parts in a theatre production. When I did see Siobhan, she barely said anything. It was fine. I was appreciative of the silence, I was getting sick of the 'I'm sorry for your loss', 'I'm thinking of you all', and 'You're in my prayers.'

I didn't see them leave or hear them say goodbye, I just continued to sit and wait, for what I don't know. After a while, my father simply put one hand on my shoulder and said, 'It's time.' I didn't ever find out if he meant it was time to leave, or if it was time to say goodbye – anyway, I didn't feel ready to do either.

I'm sure over the next week or two, life will begin to resemble normality for those around us. But not for us. We had just endured the hardest time in our lives and we're now trying to stay afloat, not drown. Perhaps we're survivors.

I watched this show once on television about a group of strangers who got dropped off on an island somewhere in the Pacific, and cameras would follow them around as they tried to find ways off the island. One guy tried to build a raft using banana leaves and bamboo, and a woman tried to signal for help to helicopters by stealing people's clothes to make into a 'Help' sign. In the end, it was the guy who did nothing who won. He simply learned how to fish and how to boil water so it was safe to drink. He even made himself a little hut to sleep in at night. He did nothing but learned how to survive – not how to escape – and won a lot of money. Really it wasn't that good a show, but Olivia and I would always watch it together on Monday nights. We would sit cross-legged on the sofa with cups of tea and biscuits and watch the show every Monday – but not this Monday.

This Monday we'd be at home, together but not really together. Maybe not even in the same room. My dad will be downstairs, somewhere near the phone in case the police call with updates. My mum will be in her bedroom with the door closed, thinking no one can hear her crying. But we can.

Sheila, our family liaison officer, left yesterday. I guess she'd tried to help Mum out by doing a wash, but she'd accidentally washed Olivia's cardigan. Mum yelled at her in the kitchen, ripped the cardigan out of her hands and told her to leave. She hadn't come back since then.

Nobody wants anything to change around here.

Some things we can't control.

Like my birthday. It's today. I'm sixteen. But I'm sure I won't be blowing out any candles today or opening any presents while family and friends clap and cheer.

No, that won't be my birthday this year. Or any other year probably.

How do you celebrate another year getting older when that means in two more years, I will be the age Olivia was when she died. And in three years,

I'll be older than her, and no longer her little sister. And maybe in ten or fifteen years, I'll be married with kids.

I'll be living my life, getting older, growing up. I'll be accomplishing things that Olivia never will.

Each birthday will remind me of what both she and I lost that day. And what we'll never get back.

I tiptoe downstairs, past the framed photos of Olivia and I together, until my feet touch the bottom. My mum is sitting in the kitchen with a cup of tea in her hands. Her face is red and puffy like she's been crying.

I just don't know how to help those around me. I don't know how to help myself.

'Mum?'

She looks up and tries to smile, but she can't.

I edge closer to her and place my arm around her shoulders. She doesn't react. She doesn't remember it's my birthday. And I don't remind her.

'How are you doing, Mum?'

'I'm fine.'

'Fine.' A response I know all too well, and use myself quite often. How does a person feel after their loved one has been murdered? Fine.

What else can we feel?

Devastated?

Angry?

Full of hatred?

No one really likes to hear that. So 'fine' is the best we can do at a time like this.

'Mrs Morrison dropped off a quiche today. Can I cut you a piece?'

'No,' she mutters. 'I'm not really hungry.'

'Yeah, me neither.'

I walk over to stand beside her and lean on the counter like she's doing, elbows propped up, I rest my chin on my hands, like her. I hear her breathing. It's slow and shallow, like she's not really breathing at all, just pretending.

'Mum?'

'Hmm?'

'Will we move after this all ends?'

'Why would you ask?'

'I mean, are we really going to stay in this house, on this island, after what happened?'

She stands up and faces me, 'Of course we are. This is Olivia's home. Why would we leave?' Cup of tea still in her hands, she turns away and heads back upstairs to her bedroom, where she will likely remain for the rest of the day and maybe tomorrow too.

This isn't Olivia's home. Not any more. *She's not here*, I want to say. I want to scream after her, *I'm here! I'm still alive!* But I don't know how to.

I'm disappearing right before their eyes. Soon I'll be nothing. A distant memory. A reminder of the family we used to have. Part of the past, not of the future.

I run upstairs but I don't go into my room, I go into Olivia's. It's cold. All the warmth has been stripped clean, like she was never here to begin with.

My body hits the bed, and I push my face into her pillow. Can I still smell her perfume? I can't. I can't smell anything any more. And soon the pillow is filled with the salty remnants of my tears.

I slide down off the bed onto the floor and grip the rug with my fingers. My hands glide over the wool and I imagine her footsteps on the fabric, toenails painted pink. I curl my knees up to my chest and rest my chin down.

My hand reaches for her bedside cabinet and I pull open the bottom drawer. Inside are a couple of magazines, some tear-outs from a travel brochure, a fabric bookmark with an elephant on it and a small tube of hand cream. I squeeze a little into my palm and rub it over my skin slowly. Thick, it covers my hands and fingers. It smells of honey and citrus.

I glance up at the door. I don't know how my mum and dad would feel if they found me in here going through her drawers. Would they be angry at me? I don't know. I don't know how they'd react. I don't seem to know them as much as I used to. They probably don't know me any more. We've all changed.

I gently coax open the top drawer and suddenly feel the room get colder. I scoop up what I found and slide back down to my knees, letting it rest on my lap. It's a small wrapped gift. And it's addressed to me. It's my birthday gift. It's the last birthday gift I'll ever get from my sister. My last birthday with her.

She chose blue wrapping and gold ribbon. She'd

tied the ribbon around twice and knotted it. She'd even curled the ends with scissors so they spiralled into ringlets. She'd written on the tag – a star – in blue pen.

Happy Birthday Alex,
I hope this will make you want to visit me now!
    Lots of love and cuddles, Liv x

Slowly removing the ribbon, the smooth cold fabric between my fingers, I gently untuck one edge of the wrapping paper and slide the content out. It's a book, hardcover with a glossy cover. Inside the book is a dried pink rose, flattened between two pages. On one of the pages she'd circled a section on rare wildflowers in Colne Valley, near London. She also starred a paragraph on Surrey Hills. I've never heard of these places before. She was inviting me to come visit her. She wanted me there with her. She would miss me, as much as I missed her.

I hope this will make you want to visit me now!

Did she think I wouldn't visit her without another reason? Wasn't she reason enough? Did she doubt me?

When I lay the book down, I see a small white corner sticking out from the pages. It's a photo of us that we took with her Polaroid. It's not really clear, like with the digital cameras you get now, but to me it's perfect. The white edges act as a mount for the photo, highlighting the image inside.

Our faces are pressed together in the photo, our cheeks touching. We're laughing, our eyes are thin slits. I press the photo to my chest and close my eyes.

Thank you, Olivia. Thank you for my birthday present. I love it.

I bring it into my room, and slide it under my pillow to look at again later. When I get downstairs my dad is making tea in the kitchen.

'Hi, Dad.'

He looks up and smiles softly at me.

'Where were you?'

He sighs. 'Just walking.'

Olivia and Dad always went for walks together. Sometimes they were gone for two or three hours. I never went with them. I don't know why now. Maybe they didn't ask me. Maybe I didn't want to. Now I do. I want to walk beside my father like my sister did. I want to talk to him openly and honestly like she did. I want us to be as close as they were. I don't want to replace her. But I want us to get through this together, not apart like we have been.

I open my mouth to tell him, to ask him if we can walk together one day. But the words don't come out that easily.

'What's that?' I finally ask, pointing to a small square cardboard box on the counter, by the stove.

'I don't know. The detective dropped it off – DI Birkens. He said it was for you.'

The lid slowly pops open, the tag sliding out of the clip that keeps it sealed. Inside is a cupcake. A white cupcake with white frosting. And on the top is a candle.

I smile and look up at my dad, but he's already gone.

Chapter Fourteen: 12.01.2016

The phone rings early the next morning. Or maybe it's later in the morning. We don't really keep track of time any more. It hasn't been kind to us, letting each day pass too quickly before our eyes but not getting us any closer to the truth about what happened to my sister.

Time taunts us. It reminds us of the lost days, and of the moments we will never get back. I hate time.

My parents' bedroom door is still closed so I lift the phone that's mounted on the wall in the hallway and carry the cordless receiver into my bedroom. I let it ring one more time before I answer it.

'Hello?'

'Yes, Hi. My name is Mark. I'm from the *Orcadian* newspaper. Is your mum or dad in?'

'Um, no. They're still sleeping, I think.'

'OK, well I can give you my number and –'

'Are you a reporter?'

'Yes, I am. But I can't talk to you.'

'Why not?' The line crackles slightly; it must be a bad signal on my end.

'Because you're still a minor and I can't interview you without your parents' consent.'

'Oh.'

'Why, would you want to be interviewed if I could?'

'No, I mean yes. I don't know. Yes, I would if it would help find my sister's killer.'

Killer. The word sounds strange out loud. Like it's not real. Like it's in a plot on a television show. Killer. Murderer. Those are words you'd read in a script, hear on the TV, not say yourself when referring to a situation you're actually going through.

'Yeah, the investigation is moving quite slow, isn't it?'

'I just thought it would be over by now. Orkney's a small island. There can't be too many suspects.'

'I agree. Of course, it doesn't help when the lead detective on the case is an alcoholic who was suspended from his position in Edinburgh after getting into an altercation with a colleague.'

'What's an altercation?'

'A fight.'

'Like a real fight? Throwing punches and all?'

'Yes, his supervisor had to physically drag him off the other guy. He could have killed him.'

'Wow. I didn't know that. I wonder if my mum and dad know? Why didn't anyone tell us?'

DI Birkens could have killed someone himself? So we have one violent man searching for another violent man? How does that even work?

'Look, your mum and dad get the *Orcadian* delivered, right?'

'Yeah, I think so.'

'Well, take a look for yourself. It's all in there.'

'Did you write it?'

'Yes, I did. I also wrote the piece on the music teacher.'

'What about the music teacher?'

'Let's just say, I think we have our suspect. Go on, take a look. You'll probably learn more from our investigation then you will from the police's. You know the saying, if you want something done right, do it yourself . . . take care now, goodbye.'

'Yeah, bye,' I mutter. I replace the handset onto the wall mount and rush downstairs.

Even though dawn still breaks outside our window, the post has already been delivered. And so have the newspapers. Gathering up what I can, I cradle the mail in my arms and let it spill out on the kitchen counter. I snatch up all the newspapers and disappear back into my bedroom before my parents wake up.

Scooting back up on my bed, I push back until my spine touches the wall and unfold the first newspaper.

Drunk Detective Fumbling Through Case.

My eyes frantically skim each letter, word, sentence until I absorb the whole article. He is a drunk. He did assault his colleague at work, which got him suspended. He and his wife are separated. And there's even something in there about a missing son. I didn't know Birkens had a child. What happened to him?

And if Birkens can't even find his own son, how is he going to find the killer of my sister?

When I devour that article, I turn to the next page. There's more.

Music Teacher's Link to Local Girl's Death.

It's talking about Olivia's music teacher, Mr Sheffield. Apparently he has a record after getting involved with an underage female student. There's a restraining order on him too by her and her parents.

My palms are clammy, and my fingers stick to the tips of the newspaper, the black ink bleeding onto my skin as I hold the paper tighter, reading each sentence over and over again.

'Stromness Academy's failure to complete a thorough background check on its staff, including David Sheffield, could have resulted in the murder of Olivia McCarthey, a female student of Sheffield's, described by sources as "just his type".'

I know Mr Sheffield. He participated in the search party through Binscarth Woods. He was in my group. He helped look for her, or pretended to. She spoke fondly of him. He even played the piano at some of her dance recitals.

I start taking inventory, going through all my inter-actions with him. He smiled at me during the search, asked me if I was OK, but maybe his eyes were lying. There was the Christmas concert last year that he played the piano in while Olivia danced. And the Christmas concerts before then. He was watching her while she danced, and now I know why.

I can see it. I can see them all. It's him. It has to be him. Who else could it be? He has a record, he had a student–teacher relationship with her, there were plenty of opportunities for something more to grow between music classes and after-school dance rehearsals.

It's him.

I have to know more.

I hear noises in the kitchen. Someone is awake.

Sliding into my jeans and a warm jumper, I step into my winter boots. My boots hit the stairs hard, and I land a little unsteadily at the bottom.

My mum peers around the corner. 'Where are you going?'

'I'm going for a walk,' I say, throwing on my coat. While I turn my body away from her, I shove the phone directory up my jumper and zip up my coat to secure it. It bulges out, but she doesn't seem to notice.

'No, you're not. You're staying here until we know what's going on out there.'

'You haven't been so bothered about what I'm doing before today? And anyway, we already know what's going on out there, Mum.' I thrust the newspapers in her hands, and start for the door.

'Alex –'

'Mum, I'm just going over to Siobhan's. I should be with my friends at a time like this, don't you think?' I hate lying to her, but she won't let me go if I tell her the truth. What am I supposed to say? 'Mum, I'm going to get the bus over to Mr Sheffield's house and look in through his windows and see if his door is unlocked so I can break in and go through his stuff and determine whether he's the killer we're all looking for? But don't worry, I'll be back in time for dinner.'

'You're right,' she says. 'Just go straight there, and come straight back. And don't stay out too late. It's a Sunday, so Siobhan will be wanting to get ready for school tomorrow. I want you back before the sun sets.'

It's a Monday. She doesn't even know it's a Monday and like my birthday, I don't remind her.

'Will do.' The door slams a little too loud behind me.

Holding the directory close to my chest, I jog lightly to the bus shelter. I don't know what number bus I'm getting but I sit on the bench and go through the S section of the phone book. There are two Sheffields listed in Orkney, so assuming he's not ex-directory, he must be one of those two.

I have to know before I just go over there. If I show up at the wrong house, they might recognize me and call the police. Then I really will be in trouble at home.

I jog to the nearest phone box, cursing my parents for not letting me have a mobile phone until my 16th birthday. Shame they forgot that was yesterday.

There's one down by the park where Olivia and I used to play when we were kids. Our bodies would curl around the slide as we went down and down until our feet touched the ground. Sometimes dad would wait at the bottom and catch us before we dropped. After the slide, we would go on the seesaw. Olivia would bounce up and down with her feet to make it go higher and higher until it jerked at the top. I would scream and we would laugh.

Once it jerked so hard at the top that I slipped and banged my chin on the safety handle and split the skin slightly. I fell off, my body hitting the rubber mat underneath. Olivia was so scared. She ran all the way home to get Mum. She promised she'd be back and she did come back. She took care of me, protected me.

After that day, she didn't go so hard on the seesaw any more. She'd gently rock up and down and when I'd ask her to go higher and harder, she'd laugh and say, 'Not today, little sister.'

When I reach the red phone box I tuck my body inside. A weird smell circles around me. I put a 20p into the slot and dial the first Sheffield on the page.

It rings and rings, and after the fourth ring a woman picks up.

'Hello?' she says.

I cough and deepen my voice until I sound like a

cartoon character off the television. 'Is Mr Sheffield home?'

'No, he's at work . . . who is this? Is this those damn newspapers again? Are you a journalist? No, my husband is not him. You have the wrong number.' And she hangs up.

So I try the next one. My next 20p snakes around inside then pops out the bottom. I slot it back in again. Again, it curls around and comes out the bottom where the change falls out. It's the only 20p I have. I have to use it. This time I push it in harder. It drops and lands on what sounds like a big pile of other coins. I wonder how much money is in there, just sitting inside.

Fingers trembling, wondering who will pick up this time, I dial the next number on the list. The last number. After this I can only assume Mr Sheffield – the real Mr Sheffield – is not listed in this directory. A man like that would probably want to stay private. If I had his past, that criminal record, I would want to stay hidden too.

But why come here? Why try and teach again? Perhaps he thought it was a small island and no one would find out? But we did. We know. We all know. It's him. He killed my sister and I'm going to make sure he's locked up forever.

It's ringing. It's still ringing. I hear a crackle and then silence.

'Hello?' I say. 'Is anybody there?'

'Who is this?'

I don't know whether to lie or tell the truth. 'I'm

calling to speak to Mr Sheffield. Is this the Mr Sheffield that works at Stromness Academy?'

'Oh god, are you a journalist? You're a bit young, aren't you? Look, you can't hound me like this! I'll press charges if you don't leave me alone. Stop calling me. No comment. I'm not going to do any interviews!'

And he hangs up.

That was him. That was the real Mr Sheffield. He's not at the police station being interrogated. He's not in a jail cell locked up so he can't harm other people. He's out. He's free. He's at home.

And he's answering the phone.

Chapter Fifteen: 12.01.2016

I slam the doors open and see the secretary drop her magazine. She yells at someone behind her, someone that I can't see. 'She's back.'

Birkens comes to the window and looks out at me. 'It's fine, Mhairi. I'll take this.'

I shuffle to the window and clear my throat loudly. 'You haven't been returning my calls.'

The wooden doors click open and I march over and slide through. I find Birkens standing there with his arms crossed. 'I've told you this before. You coming down here every day is just delaying the investigation. You can't be here right now. What happened with Sheila? –'

'Why is he not here? Why is he at home?'

'Who?'

'Mr Sheffield!'

'How do you know about Mr Sheffield?' says Allans, as he approaches from behind me.

'Dave,' warns Birkens.

'See? I knew it! He *is* a suspect!'

'Lower your voice, please. Who have you been talking to?' he asks.

'I don't need to talk to anyone because it's all over the newspapers!'

Birkens nods and shifts his weight, placing his hands on his hips.

'Well? Do something about it! Why aren't you out there arresting him?'

'We can't do that.'

'Did you even question him?'

'I can't disclose details of the investigation –'

'Why not? Everyone else is! I read all about the investigation in the newspaper. I didn't even know he was a suspect! He has a record! It's him, I know it is!'

'He's not a suspect . . .' Birkens takes a deep breath and rubs his forehead. 'Look, when we know something, you'll know something.'

I shake my head, 'What do you care anyway? This case probably means nothing to you. Just another murder, right? One of many for you? Murders might happen every week in a big city like Edinburgh, but they don't happen here. Maybe if you weren't drinking –'

'That's not fair –' interjects Allans.

'This is my sister! Nothing's fair!'

'I understand your loss,' Birkens says quietly.

'I know you do. I read about that too in the newspaper. Your son, was it?'

He looks at me, his cheeks a little flushed. He opens

his mouth then closes it again. Perhaps I've crossed a line. Perhaps I don't even know where the line is any more. Everything is so blurred now, so unfamiliar.

Birkens takes a cautious step forward, and unfolds his arms, letting his hands drop heavily by his sides. 'I understand your frustrations. I'm just asking you to let us do our job. Please.'

'Fine,' I eventually say. I start walking back towards the door. 'But we want some answers. We're entitled to that. We deserve to know what's going on!'

Dusk blankets my street by the time I return home. Soft grey and pink hues flow over the rooftops and fences. Seagulls squabble and snap at each other somewhere behind me, beyond the row of houses. Television sets flicker against the windows, each house lighting up like bulbs on a string of fairy lights.

The street is silent, disturbed by nothing, not even the rumbling of a car engine. I look out towards the sea, as if I can see it beyond the walls and doors that face me. I imagine staring at the water, the waves flowing gently over each other. Dipping, rocking, crashing. I want to go down, sit for a while on the sand and pebbles, and feel the cold breeze take hold of me. But I don't have the freedom to wander any more.

It's not safe here.

A twinge tickles my belly, deep down. An unfamiliar feeling of something that I don't recognize but that I saw in Olivia every day.

For the first time in my life, I feel . . . trapped. Maybe

even a little suffocated. A cold shiver shoots up my spine and my shoulders tremble slightly. I hope the feeling passes. It has to pass. This is my home, the place I never wanted to leave behind.

I shuffle up to my house and up the steps. My hand grips the edge of the doorway, as I take a deep breath in and out.

It will pass.

The front door is locked so I use my key and slip in quietly so no one can hear me. I should have been back long before the sun has started to set. I hope my parents aren't mad. I don't want to upset them further.

But when I move inside, I don't see them waiting for me. The kitchen lights are on, and the kettle boils softly in the background. I move further into the house and listen for my parents. I hear them. Their muffled voices seep out under the living room door into the hallway. Pressing my ear against the door, I listen to them talk.

'I don't understand, Peter. Why didn't she tell us her and James had broken up?'

'I don't know.'

'She never lied about anything. She always came home when she said she would. We always knew where she was. We had no reason to doubt her, or worry about her. But I don't think we really knew what she was up to these last few months. I don't think we knew our daughter at all.'

'Don't say that. We knew her, we did. We're not bad parents –'

'Then why didn't she confide in us? Why would she hide things?'

'Do you think Alex knew?'

'I don't know. Would she even tell us now?'

'Do you think she's doing OK?'

'How should I know? She barely says two words to us now.'

'I don't like her out and about outside. She should be here, inside where it's safe.'

'You don't really think whoever did this is still out there, do you?'

'I don't know, maybe.'

'He's gone. We won't find him. No one will. If he was going to be found, it would have happened already. But we're in the same situation we were when Olivia first went missing. The police know nothing. We know nothing. The only person who does know something is probably already off this island. He's probably in Spain or Portugal or something. He's probably laughing at us, and how we chased our tails for weeks!'

'Keep your voice down, Peter.'

'He got away with it. He knows that. Now I'm beginning to understand why.'

'Good old-fashioned police work,' says my mum, her voice trembling.

'They don't know what they're doing. And this so-called Detective Inspector Birkens is the worst. He doesn't keep us updated, he doesn't call. We read about any new leads or information in the newspaper. And now this?'

'I know. I saw it. And I think Alex did too.'

'A drunk? Violent? Suspended from his last job? Who hired him? And who assigned him to my daughter's case?'

I hear rustling and a zipper scratching.

'Where are you going?' she asks.

'I'm going to speak to Birkens. I want to hear what he has to say about all this!'

The living room swings open and my dad is standing there in the doorway, with his coat and gloves on.

'When did you get back?' he asks.

Before I can open my mouth to answer, the doorbell rings, making me jump. A tall broad silhouette fills the window, his details hidden by the frosted tint and red rose design that snakes all the way up the glass. My dad reaches for the door handle and pushes it down. A gust of wintery wind slips in.

Detective Inspector Birkens stands on the step, his short hair blowing gently in the wind. Dark circles around his eyes, skin slightly sagging. I hadn't noticed how drained he looked before.

'Can I come in?' he asks.

My dad opens the door wider, and Birkens steps in, closing it behind him. He looks at me, eyebrows raised, but doesn't say anything about my station visit or the outburst.

We all shuffle into the living room, and find my mum

still sitting in the armchair. She rises when she sees Birkens come in. 'Detective, I didn't know you were coming. Can I get you a tea or coffee?'

'No, thank you. I'm not staying long.' He sits in the chair opposite her, and my dad and I sit on the middle sofa, our heads cranked towards him. 'I know by now, you've probably read the papers and turned on the television and I wanted to speak about what's out there.' He shifts uncomfortably in the chair. 'Firstly, we did interview Mr Sheffield –'

'Why didn't we know you had a suspect?' asks my dad.

'Because he wasn't a suspect. And he isn't one –'

'He has a record! He has a history of developing relationships with female students!' snaps my mum.

'He was guilty of that, and he was charged at the time. His teaching licence was suspended. A background check was not completed on him by the school and he was hired at Stromness Academy. But he has had a clean record since.'

'That makes no difference!'

'You're right,' says Birkens. 'But he's not responsible for Olivia's death. And that's why we did not make any arrests.'

'How do you know for sure he didn't do this?' asks my mum.

'Because he was performing at the Kirkwall Hogmanay Festival from 9 p.m. until 1.00 a.m. with his band. Most of the 120 guests confirmed that. He then went on to one of the pubs, where his time of entry and exit was also confirmed. He did not leave Kirkwall that evening to get back to Stromness to kill Olivia.'

'He could have done it after?'

'No, the autopsy confirms that Olivia suffered a fatal head injury on the night of the 31st.'

'But she didn't die then?'

Birkens shakes his head. 'We're still waiting on more information from the pathologist we brought in. We'll know more soon.'

'What about the rose left at the funeral?' I ask.

'We did ask around, and no one says they left it or saw anybody carrying a red rose at the funeral. And the only prints I lifted off it were yours and mine.'

'Oh.' I slide back on the sofa, until my spine hits the cushion behind me, and glance at my mum and dad, wondering who will ask the next question.

My dad clears his throat. 'And what of the other allegations?' His tone is low and cautious.

Birkens sits back in the chair and crosses one leg over the other. 'I do have a past. Most people do. There was an incident in Edinburgh, but don't believe everything that you read in the newspapers. Just trust that I am capable of doing the job and finding the person who murdered your daughter.'

My parents exchange looks, and my dad nods slowly like he accepts the explanation, asking for no more. I still have a lot of questions, but perhaps it's not my place, or my business, to ask right now. I want to know more about his son, about what happened to him, and more importantly, why he couldn't find him.

I don't want Olivia lost like him. I can't not know.

Birkens is looking at me. He wants my approval too. He wants me to say everything is OK, that I believe him, that I trust him to do this.

'OK,' I finally say.

'OK,' he responds.

Chapter Sixteen: 13.01.2016

The letter came through four days ago. It wasn't really addressed to anyone specific, more to the whole family. What's left of my family anyway. A memorial for Olivia at school. 'A chance for her peers to say goodbye.' Wasn't the funeral for that? Are there more goodbyes to be said?

Honestly, I don't think I can take any more goodbyes. I've said it too much. And each time, it still seems wrong, still seems premature. Because I don't think we can really say goodbye properly until this person is caught. Until this is solved.

But here I am. Back at school for this memorial. To say goodbye. Again.

I'm standing at the front door. I haven't even made it inside yet. On the door is a black and white photocopy of my sister's face. Her smiling expression stops me from going inside. Because I know she's not smiling now. And never will again.

The car park is full. Cars line up against each other like soldiers on a battlefield. One after another. Waiting. Like me. Maybe even *for* me.

What will I say when I get inside? Will I be expected to stand up and say something into a microphone?

I don't know why I'm here. I just know someone in my family had to come and be here tonight and that person seemed to be me. Mum was upstairs in her bedroom crying when I left. And dad was sitting downstairs in the living room, TV off, just staring into the fireplace. The flames snaked high across the bricks, and crackled against the spark guard. And my dad just stared. As if he saw something that we didn't.

Out of both my parents, I worry about my dad more. My mum cries and at least gets it out. My dad doesn't do any of that. He doesn't cry. He doesn't scream. He doesn't get angry and smash things. He's quiet. He stares a lot at the wall, or the fireplace, and even sometimes at Olivia's closed bedroom door.

He just looks . . . broken.

And I don't know what to do about that. I don't know how to help him. I don't know if he even wants help at this point or if he just wants to be left alone.

I look up again at my sister's face.

Who did this to you, Olivia?

Why?

I can't go in. I can't face those people. What if the killer is one of them? What if he's there waiting for me?

I can hear noise from within. Movement of feet, chairs scraping, voices. I'm late. It's 6.10 p.m. I was supposed to be here for 6.00 p.m. I've been standing outside for ten minutes, just staring at the door, at her picture. Like my dad, I guess. I wonder if he's moved from the sofa? I wonder if the flames have died down yet. If he'll tend to them or not even notice the fire is out.

I see her face. It's staring back at me. It's haunting me. It's not her. She's not here. She's not inside. She's gone. She's nothing now. Not even a flicker of an existence.

I should leave. I shouldn't be here.

'Are you going to go in or just keep standing there?'

I spin round and see Birkens leaning against the wall like he's been there for a while.

'Well, come on then. Let's do it together, shall we?' he says. He walks in front of me, opens the front door, Olivia's face disappearing around the corner, and gestures me inside.

I don't want to go in, but I do. I feel safer with him here. I feel braver.

Inside, the hallways are empty, vacant of students. But beyond that, beyond the classrooms, are dozens and dozens of people in the assembly hall. Actually, not dozens, maybe hundreds. Everyone from Olivia's year stands together with a red candle in their hands, lit, the flame flickering up towards the ceiling. The rest of the students seem to be from different years, different ages. They stand with each other. They stand together.

On the wall in front is a slide-down projector showing pictures of Olivia in school. She's sitting in class with Emily. She's dancing in the end-of-year summer concert. She's sitting at the lunch table with James holding hands. She's everywhere. And yet nowhere.

I turn to Birkens to see if he's still there. He is. Of course he is. He's right beside me.

'I don't think I can –'

'Yes you can' he says, motioning towards the middle of the room.

When I get there, people move aside for me, a path opening up before me. Siobhan finds me and hugs me hard. She pushes my hair to the side and whispers in my ear, 'Please talk to me.'

But I'm empty inside. I have nothing left to say to these people.

In the middle are chairs. I sit.

The lights dim slightly, and everyone else sits too. And then there's silence.

Candles flicker all around me. Her face is behind me, next to me, in front of me.

I can't breathe.

Birkens is suddenly next to me, and now I can breathe.

I listen as Olivia's friends, her peers, and even those who knew her but never really knew her, stand up and talk about her. They tell stories I've never heard, share jokes I never laughed at, and talk about people I don't know.

This is *their* Olivia.

There are memories I was never – and will never – be a part of.

I'm not the only one who lost her. I'm not the only one who's missing her. And I'm definitely not the only one who wants who did this dead.

I feel sadness in the room, even fear, but most of all – anger.

They're angry – no, *we're* angry.

We're in this together. I'm not alone. I'm finally not alone in this.

When it's over, I thank as many people as I can. I shake hands, exchange hugs, and even cry with strangers. But they're not strangers to me, not any more. They're friends.

Thank you.

I needed this.

After, I go outside. I need to feel the cold air on my face to know I'm still here, I'm still alive. But when I get outside and walk around the corner towards the football pitch, I see Emily leaning against the brick wall with a cigarette in her hand. It's amber-hued at the tip, and dropping little golden flecks onto the ground below.

'Emily?'

She startles and drops her cigarette. 'Sorry,' she says and fumbles around for it.

When she stands up, her face is red, blotchy.

'Are you OK?'

She laughs nervously, 'I should be asking you that.'

'We're doing fine,' I robotically say. Good response for everything.

'Yeah, well I'm not,' she says, wiping her tears from

her hands. 'Shit' she cries, as the cigarette burns her cheek slightly. 'Sorry, I don't know why this is harder for me than the funeral.'

'For me it's easier.'

'Good,' she smiles. 'Alex, I'm sorry I haven't been round much. I . . .' She starts crying, harder this time. She tries to speak to me but I can't understand her words. Her back shakes and she eventually covers her face with her hands, dropping the cigarette on the ground. 'I just feel so guilty.'

'I hear you had a fight with Olivia right before she –'

'It was so stupid. I was so stupid.'

'It wasn't your fault.'

'It was! I overheard her silly conversation with her new boyfriend and I was so obsessed over her not telling me, that I wasn't thinking. She didn't have to tell me everything. But I thought she did. I was just offended, that's all.'

'What new boyfriend?'

'I guess she was seeing someone new. Whoever it was, was calling her over and over that night. She was leaving to go meet him and I got . . . I don't know . . . jealous, I think. We were there together. This was our last Hogmanay before she went to London and all she wanted to do was spend it with a guy. She was leaving for London in only a few months, and she didn't give a shit that I wasn't coming.'

'Emily, wait, who was this new boyfriend? Who was she meeting that night?'

'I don't know. She wouldn't tell me his name.'

'Does he go to school?'

'I don't know. I didn't meet him, but I don't think so.'

'Why? Why don't you think so?'

She shrugs and roughly pushes her coat collar up to shield her neck from the cold air.

'Was he younger? Maybe he's in my year?'

'Maybe. I don't know. But she said he had a car and was driving to meet her. I don't know many fifteen-year-olds who can drive, right?'

'Did you find out anything else?'

'No, nothing. She was being really secretive and that's why we fought.'

'Did you tell the detective this?'

'Olivia made me promise not to tell anyone.'

'Emily, this is serious! This could have been the last person to see her alive. We have to find him.' I turn to start walking back to the gym. I have to find Birkens.

'Alex!' she calls after me.

I turn to see her standing there, the lights from the car park glowing from behind her. Her car keys clutched in her hand, so tight I can barely see them. 'My last words to her were "I hate you", did you know that?'

I shake my head. 'Well, I don't even remember my last words to her, so I don't know what's worse.'

I turn away from her so she can't see the tears fall down my cheeks. I pick up speed until I get back to the gym. It's still busy. No one is leaving. I don't see James – he left without even saying goodbye.

I take a deep breath and find Birkens by the chairs. He's staring straight ahead, like my dad. But I can't tell who he's looking at, or what he's thinking. His stare is empty, filled with nothing.

And just like my dad, he too looks broken.

Chapter Seventeen: 14.01.2016

I get to Birkens' house by late morning. I couldn't talk to him at the memorial. I tried to, but when I finally pushed through the crowd to him, he was gone. After that, it was too late to call him.

I had called the station at 10.20 a.m. but they said that Birkens was working from home today. So, here I am, but he's not answering the front door. I knock loudly. His car is here, so he must be home. Why isn't he answering?

I push the door open and walk into the entryway. It's small, and has a thin red plaid rug over the wooden flooring. The walls are bare, as if no one lives here. I call his name, softly at first but then a little louder. Silence greets me.

I keep walking and find the kitchen at the bottom of the hallway, and there I find Birkens sitting in an armchair by the window in the kitchen. He doesn't see me at first. He looks different today. Older. More fatigued. A little more broken. The whisky bottle slams down on the table as he fills another glass. Droplets slide down from the neck of the bottle, forming a circular stain on the dusty wooden table underneath when he puts it down. He rubs his forehead as if it throbs and pulses. Still not aware I'm standing there, I watch him reach over and slide open a drawer in front of him. He rummages around for a moment, paper clips and small envelopes spilling out onto the floor, then eventually pulls out a small white tube-like container.

He shakes the bottle and tiny pebbles or capsules thrash against the sides like a rainstick. He pops open the lid and coaxes out three round pills. He tosses them into his mouth, and takes a long gulp from his glass. He puts the lid back on, and throws them back into the drawer, kicking it closed with his foot. He leans back into his chair.

I shouldn't be here. Gently stepping back, I ease towards the door.

He sits up, back straight then spins around. 'Alex. I didn't hear you come in. Did you ring the bell?'

I keep backing up towards the door. 'I . . . I . . . your door was open, so I just walked in. I'm really sorry. I can tell you're busy.'

He stands up and starts to straighten his shirt, tucking it in around the edges of his grey trousers. He smoothes his hair with his hands, and reaches for his dark navy tie. 'I was just . . .' He looks at me, then his eyes quickly dart down to the floor and back up to meet mine. He coughs and clears his throat. 'So, what can I do for you?'

I don't know what to say. Suddenly I don't know why I'm standing here in his kitchen. I should have waited until tomorrow when he came back to work. Or maybe I came for a different reason.

All I know is that Birkens appears to be swaying as he stands before me. This is the man who stood in the station and asked me to trust him to do his job?

I walk over to the kettle and start filling it at the sink. 'Tea?' I ask.

'No, not for me, thanks.'

'Coffee then?'

'No. What time is it?' he says, sitting back down in the chair.

'Not too early for whisky, apparently.' I rinse two coffee mugs and sit them by the kettle. 'Sugar?'

'Not in mine, please. If you want it, it's in the cupboard above the toaster. Probably at the back of the shelf since I never use it.'

The steam from the kettle rises up and fills the air with warm mist. It's wintery outside, but a musty smell sits in the kitchen and turns my stomach, so I lean over and open the latch on the window by the sink. Cold air rushes in but the scent is refreshing.

The kettle finally clicks, and I pour two mugs – one with strong black coffee and the other with milky tea. Taking the glass of whisky in one hand, I replace it with the coffee mug on the table before him. He reaches up and stops me from leaving, gently taking back the whisky. He doesn't drink it though, just rests it down in front of him beside the coffee, as if he can't let it go, not just yet.

'Why do you carry around a Superman keyring?'

He doesn't respond.

'I saw it at the hospital. You were holding it in your hand while you sat and waited for me to wake up. Why?'

He pauses, and looks down at his shoes as if he doesn't want to answer my questions. So I wait in silence, hoping he'll say something, anything, to distract me from own thoughts, the ones that burn in my mind and scratch away at the memories I have of my sister.

'My son gave it to me for my birthday one year. He'd got it at Alton Towers, I think. I held on to it after . . . after I left Edinburgh.'

'Why did you leave? I can't imagine anyone leaving a big city like Edinburgh for a small place like this. Olivia was going to move to London. Did you know?'

'Yes, I did know.'

'Right, that's your job I guess. To know everything about my sister.'

I look around the room. It's small, with a sink by the window and white-washed wooden shelves in the corner filled with books and an 8x10 frame. It has a photo of a boy in it, someone I don't recognize – it must be his son.

'Is that why you drink?' I ask him. 'Because of my sister? Because you're worried you won't be able to catch the person who killed her? Or that he'll do it again?'

'No.' He takes a deep breath and stares into his glass.

'Don't misunderstand me, of course I'm worried about finding your sister's killer. But I know we will. I don't drink because of that. No, I've been drinking for longer than that. Probably for four years now.'

He sits back in his armchair. He's looking at something beyond me, beyond these walls, and it seems to be the time when I can finally ask him. 'What happened to your son, Detective?'

Then he starts talking, but I don't know to whom because he's not looking at me. He's not looking at anyone, just a shadow behind me. 'I was at the playground. My wife was finishing her shift at the hospital. Ryan – my son – kept calling to me to push him on the swings, but I didn't go to him. I was so tired. I was in the middle of a case, and it was taking all I had. I could barely keep my eyes open. I leaned back on the bench, rested my head against the brick wall behind, just for a second. That's all I needed.'

Birkens picks up his glass and swirls the whisky inside it. I worry he's going to take another drink.

'I don't know how many minutes had passed before I woke up. But when I did, I knew immediately I had fallen asleep. When I looked over at the swings, he wasn't there.'

He lifts the glass to his lips, but before he takes a sip, he lowers it suddenly and puts it back on the table in front of him. He slides the glass away from him, and picks up the coffee mug. He rubs his forehead, and glances back at the framed photo of the little blond boy.

'We searched the whole area for weeks. I sent divers into the river. We ran surveillance at Edinburgh and Glasgow airports, checked video footage at train stations, bus stations. Nothing. He was gone. It was like he'd never even existed.'

'How old was he?' I finally ask, my words sounding strange, as if they belong to someone else.

'He was about to turn six. His birthday was a week after. It's today actually. He would have been ten today.'

I don't know what to say. So I say what everyone else says to me: 'I'm sorry for your loss.'

He smiles and nods his head. 'I'm sorry for yours.'

My chest aches so I stand up, and walk towards the photo of the little boy to buy me a moment to stop my eyes from watering. I don't like people seeing me cry. I'm stronger than that. I think.

I hold the frame in my hand, the boy smiling back at me. He's in the arms of a woman who wears her hair like my mum. She's smiling at him, her eyes not looking at the camera as if she doesn't even know it's there. 'Who's the woman?'

Birkens gets up and takes the frame from my fingers. He delicately places it back on the shelf, as if it were made of eggshells and might shatter in my hands. 'It's my wife, Cheryl.'

'Where is she now? Does she live in Orkney too?'

'No. She's still in Edinburgh.'

'Why is she in Edinburgh and you're here?'

'Good question.'

'Do you still talk to her?'

'She calls now and then to check in, but I rarely answer. No time . . . that's a lie, I have the time. I just don't want to talk to her. I don't know what to say.'

'You could try writing it down on paper. That might make it easier? My dad says to do that, if I have an oral presentation at school or something. He says to write down my thoughts into bullet points so I have something to read from in the moment, if I get stuck with my words.'

'That's good advice from your dad,' he smiles. The expression looks uncomfortable on him. 'You should get home now. I would drive you back but I really shouldn't be driving,' he says, gesturing over to the half-empty whisky bottle.

'That's OK. I can take the bus at the bottom of the road.' I zip my coat up to the top. I close the kitchen window, in case Birkens forgets and wakes up to a cold house.

Before I leave, I turn back and see him sliding the whisky bottle back into the cabinet under the sink. I hear a clash of glass and wonder how many bottles are under there. I hope he doesn't start drinking again after I leave.

'Mr Birkens, I mean, Detective Inspector?'

'Yes?'

'Thank you.'

'I haven't done anything yet.'

'You have,' I say, before I close the door behind me.

Chapter Eighteen: 14.01.2016

The wind creeps in under my jacket lining and slides in around the collar. It feels colder today. I rub my hands together, the thick woollen gloves scratching the tops of my fingers.

The bus is running late.

I shuffle over to the timetable, my cold jeans rubbing against my legs. These were once too tight, and now they hang loosely from my thin frame. I can't seem to stop losing weight. I can't sleep through the night either, the nightmares coming back to me over and over again.

The timetable is old, the date on it is 2014, but the times still read the same. I turn my head and see a MISSING poster of Olivia in the corner of the bus shelter. I remember coming here with my dad to put it up. We hadn't gone around to remove them after her body was found, but somehow they'd disappeared from the shelters, windows, doorways and lampposts where we'd stuck them. But this shelter had been missed.

Sliding a glove off, I reach up and gently tug at the corner. It slips down off the glass and crumples, folding over my hand.

'Alex?'

When I turn around, I see Allans in a red Honda parked in front of the shelter. His hazard lights are on, and his window is rolled all the way down.

I manage half a smile.

'Are you OK?' he asks.

'Yeah, I'm just waiting on the bus.'

'Get in. I'll give you a lift back to your house.'

The street in front of us and behind us is empty, so I climb in, not knowing if and when the bus will show up.

When I close the door, Allans rolls the window up and turns up the knob on the heat. Warmth bursts out of the side vents and quickly fills the car. It feels good on my face. I wriggle my toes and feel even my socks getting warmer.

'Freezing today, isn't it?'

I nod.

'What's that?'

I'm still holding the MISSING poster of Olivia. 'It's an old flyer, from when we were looking for my sister.'

'Oh. I didn't realize some were still up.'

'It's fine.'

He flicks on the radio. An English woman's voice spills out from the speakers around us.

'Local authorities are still at a loss as to who murdered Orkney teen Olivia McCarthey on the night of the 31st. Sources confirm the teenager suffered a fatal blow to the back of the head . . .'

'Sorry,' he mumbles, flicking to a different station. Classical music streams out, the string instruments drowning out the silence in the car. 'Sorry,' he says again.

'It's OK. It's probably on every radio channel right now.'

The car hits a dip in the road, and my shoulder bumps against the side.

'Why were you at that bus shelter anyway? A bit far from your house.'

'You remember where I live?'

'I'm a police officer. It's my job to remember facts,' he smirks. He checks the rearview mirror and clears his throat. 'Were you at the detective inspector's house?'

I know I shouldn't have been there. I don't want him to get in trouble so I lie. 'No, I was just seeing a friend who lives nearby.'

I wonder if he can see through my lie.

'You have a friend that lives by the DI's house?'

'Yep.' I need to change the subject. 'Why were you there?'

'I went out to see the detective but there was no answer at the front door. He didn't come in today so I wanted to check on him.'

'Maybe he's sick?'

The corners of his mouth raise slightly. 'Maybe.'

I lean my head against the window and watch the houses skim by one at a time. Andy lives near here somewhere. I've only been to his house once. I had gone with Siobhan one Friday night when Olivia was out with James, and my dad had been working late. My mum had gone to a craft group at her friend Mary's house down the street, so I went out and was back by the time she got home.

We hung out in Andy's bedroom. He and Siobhan drank sherry mixed with Diet Coke from his dad's cabinet, while I sipped Irn-Bru from a ceramic mug. I never did like the taste of alcohol and the feel of it in my belly. Siobhan had drunk too much, so I left Andy to walk her home while I got the bus back. I had arrived only minutes before Mum got back.

'I saw you talking with Emily Morrison at the memorial at the school last night.'

'Yeah, she's Olivia's best friend . . . I mean *was* Olivia's best friend.'

Was. Not Is. Was.

'Did she share any new information?' he asks, turning the volume down on the radio.

I open my mouth to answer then realize that if I tell Allans what she said then I won't have any reason to visit Birkens again tomorrow. And that feels weird to me. I don't know why. Maybe I just want Birkens to know that I can be useful to the investigation, that I'm not a child. I can help. And if he thinks that I can help then maybe he'll start sharing information with me.

'No, not really,' I say, looking back out the window so he doesn't see my cheeks flush. My face burns red when I lie. Mum told me that years ago, so I stopped lying. Not that I needed to much, but after that I found ways to creatively *omit* information, without having to lie. That's all I'm doing now. Omitting the information until I tell Birkens myself.

We turn the corner and I see my house up ahead. My dad's car sits in the driveway. Allans pulls up and as I lift the latch to open the passenger door, he places a hand gently on my forearm. 'Look, maybe you were there to visit a "friend", or maybe you were there to see the DI. I just want you to be careful. You've seen the newspapers. We all have. DI Birkens is a good detective, but the investigation is moving slower than we expected and we don't have any new leads. Any new information you have or find out later, I just want you to know that you can come to me any time. Birkens isn't from here. I am, born and raised. Finding the person who killed your sister – a local – is my priority. Birkens has . . . other priorities on his mind right now.'

'I trust him,' I say. 'He'll find this person.'

Allans lifts his hand, and shifts back into his seat. 'I hope so.'

I slam the car door a little too hard behind me, and hurry into the house, hearing Allans' car pull away from the street.

*

I skip dinner, and instead fall asleep in front of the TV. At some point my dad switches it off, and either carries me or shuttles me half asleep to my bedroom. He pulls the covers up over my shoulders, and closes the door tight. But it doesn't stay closed for long.

Because every night, my mum comes into my bedroom. I don't know when, and I don't know why. I always pretend to be asleep, and I think maybe deep down she knows I'm pretending, but she doesn't say my name, or try and wake me. She leaves me be. I feel her weight on the covers beside me, sinking my body deeper down into the mattress. She sits beside me, not too close, not too far away. And she gently puts her hand on my head. She delicately but carefully strokes my head as I lie there with my eyes closed, but my mind racing.

Her palm is the perfect temperature. Not too cool to the touch, and not burning with heat on my forehead. It's always been lukewarm, just enough coolness, just enough warmth. She sits for about a half hour, night after night, doing this. And I wouldn't want it any other way.

But come morning, when the sun breaks through, she's gone. And when I see her later in the day, it's like she was never there. I want to ask why she comes. I want to ask her why she doesn't talk to me about it when we're both awake and when the house is filled with light streaming in from the windows. But the words don't come so easily, to both she and I.

Tonight the light from the lampposts outside flickers on my bedroom wall. I squeeze the pillow closer and tuck any loose fabric under my chin. It must be in my head, but the pillowcase still feels damp from my tears the night before.

The bedroom door clicks open and I know it's her again. My mum. Coming to sit beside me in silence, coming to stroke my hair and tell me everything is going to be OK even though her mouth never opens to speak.

The bed sinks a little, and I feel her body warmth beside me. Her hand is on my head, and she's stroking my hair. Again, like every night, I close my eyes tight and pretend to sleep. But tonight, I can't. Tonight, I want to know.

So I open my eyelids slowly and turn to her. She looks surprised and stops touching my head. She slides away from me a little, and quietly murmurs, 'Sorry.'

I touch her arm, so she doesn't leave and she seems to startle at my touch.

'You don't have to go,' I say.

She smiles, the corners of her mouth flickering slightly. 'And you don't have to fake sleeping.'

'Deal.'

Her hand is back on my hair, and she's brushing the loose strands along my hairline away from my forehead. 'How long have you known I've come in?'

'Every night.'

'Why didn't you say?'

'Why didn't you?'

Her hand stops moving and she rests it back in her lap. She tips her head and looks up out of the window, at the frosty streets and snow-capped rooftops, at the people sleeping in their beds, at the fireplaces still crackling from the evening before. 'Every night I have the same dream . . . nightmare, actually. It's a nightmare.'

I roll over more and tuck my hands under my face, tilting it up towards her.

'Olivia is in it, most nights. Some nights, it's just fragments of her – her voice, a blink of a memory, a flicker of her face. Some nights, it's not even really her, but in the nightmare I think it's her. I believe it's her. She's always close, but not quite close enough.'

Her voice breaks and I can see her eyes glimmer with the wetness of tears as the moon shines down on her face from the window.

'Then I wake up, and I remember why I'm dreaming about her. And all I want to do is come in here and see you.'

'Why?'

'I don't know. Maybe I need to remember you're still here. Maybe I'm scared one day that you won't be, that I'll lose you too.'

'I have those dreams too.'

'I didn't know.'

'If you ever want to come in here to sleep with me, I can move over. The bed is big enough for the two of us. If you want?'

She strokes my hair again, the wispy strays around my hairline always her target. She'd put a little hairspray on them to flatten them down after she'd French braid my hair when I was younger. I hated the French braid. It was so tight and so unnatural for me. But she liked it, so I let her do it. All I ever wanted to do was make her happy. And she wanted the same for us, Olivia and me. We were everything to her. And now her family's gone. 'But I'm still here,' I say, louder than I expected.

'I know, Alexandra. I know.' She leans down and kisses my forehead, her lips the same perfect temperature as her hands. And then she gets up and leaves the room, the moon still streaming in through the frosty glass.

Chapter Nineteen: 15.01.2016

The ground beneath my boots crunches and crackles as I make my way across the field. The sky begins to open up behind me and I can feel the first ray of the day's sun striking my back. A new day. Another one gone. And I feel no closer to finding the truth.

A farmer tending to a herd of sheep waves at me, loudly greeting me with a good morning. I wave back and nod. I wonder if he recognizes my face, knows who I am, who I'm related to. Or *was* related to, I guess. There it is again – Was.

We must be celebrities around here by now, Olivia's in the newspapers so much. Yesterday's headline stated 'Killer Still at Large'. As if people had forgotten. As if people needed new justification for suddenly wanting to lock their doors at night. I even saw a neighbour installing a high-tech security system the other day. Everyone is thinking the same thing – will there be more murders?

I don't know.

If so, who's next?

Me?

Clouds of dark grey smoke billow out from Birkens' chimney and I know he's already awake. I don't know what happened yesterday. I don't know what I'm going to say to him when I arrive at his door.

He's lost someone too. He knows how I feel. Maybe we're not so different after all.

A twinge hits my stomach, and I feel . . . I don't know – guilty? I shouldn't have said those things in the station. It must be difficult for him to see himself in the papers, and his son, even after all this time. To be constantly reminded of the one case he could not solve.

Maybe we won't ever find out what truly happened that night my sister was taken.

God, I hope not.

I reach his door quicker than I had hoped and then I'm standing there, fist raised, ready to knock but not ready to make contact with the door.

Suddenly it swings open, and Birkens is standing in the doorway, coat on, scarf and keys in his hand. The small Superman keyring swings from his fingers. He looks just as surprised and appears to be just as uncomfortable as me.

'Alex, what are you doing here?'

'I . . . I . . .' He looks terrible. That's all I can think right now. His hair is a mess, and I can clearly tell what side of his face was on the pillow because one side is all red and puffy. 'Yesterday I –'

'You should come in.' He opens the door wider and gestures for me to come inside.

I duck under his arm and stand in the hallway where I was just twenty-four hours ago. The major difference is that today he seems to be sober.

Motioning for me to follow, he walks into the kitchen and turns on the kettle. He slides out of his coat and lays it across the kitchen counter by the oven.

I remove mine and snuggle in to the armchair where he sat the day before. Several pale rings sit on the wooden table beside me, scars from the many glasses laid there. Hopefully not all from his hand.

'Coffee?'

I nod, even though I don't actually drink coffee.

'Sugar? Milk?'

I nod again.

The cabinet door is slightly ajar, and the edge of a glass bottle sticks out slightly. The inside liquid is an amber brown, like whisky.

The click of the kettle makes me jump, and I look up to see Birkens pouring boiling water into two ceramic mugs. One has a chipped handle.

He carries them over awkwardly and places them down in front of me. He slides the one with the chipped handle towards himself, and raises it to his mouth. I hold the other in my palms, feeling the heat warm the inside of my skin. It's still cold in here.

He puts the mug down and leans in. 'I'm sorry about yesterday. It wasn't right for you to see me like that or for me to be drinking so early in the day. You shouldn't have seen that. And I shouldn't have said those things to you.'

'It's fine, really. I shouldn't have just let myself in to your house like that. Sorry.'

He smiles. 'Well, you're here again today.'

'Yes, sorry about that too. I just really wanted to tell you what I came by yesterday to tell you.'

'OK,' he says, leaning back in his armchair.

'At the memorial on Tuesday, Emily said she and Olivia had an argument at the Hogmanay party –'

'Yes we know –'

'But she didn't tell you what about, right?'

'She said she couldn't remember.'

'It was about Olivia's new boyfriend.'

'Emily Morrison told you this?'

'Yes.'

'What new boyfriend?'

'Exactly what I'm wondering. I thought she and James were still together at the time, which we know now wasn't true. She had a new boyfriend, clearly a secret boyfriend because she didn't even tell her best friend. Emily said she heard her talking on her phone outside the party, and when she asked her about it, she admitted that she'd been seeing someone new.'

'For how long?'

'That I don't know.'

'Do you know his name?'

'No, neither does Emily.'

'Would she have confided in anyone else about him?'

'Someone other than her best friend or her sister? No, definitely not.'

'Do you think James knew about this new boyfriend.'

'I don't know. Wait, you're not still on him, are you? I thought he wasn't a suspect? Mr Sheffield is more of a suspect than James. I've known James for over four years. He would never hurt anyone.'

'Sheffield is no longer a person of interest, I told you that.'

'But are you really sure?'

'He has an alibi for that night, you know that.'

I sink back into the chair, feeling a little defeated.

'Alex, the pathologist's report told us something else too.'

'What?'

'I decided not to tell you and your parents, but now I'm afraid the report will get leaked . . . and I think you deserve to know. I know I would have wanted to know everything.'

The mug trembles in my hand, hot liquid spilling out over the edges and crawling its way down the ceramic to my fingers. He lifts the mug out of my hands, and places it on the table beside me.

'Her autopsy reveals blunt force trauma to the head –'

'I know that.'

'But the autopsy and the soil samples we took from the site confirms what we were afraid of.'

'What? Just tell me!' I can hear my voice cracking. Don't cry.

'Olivia wasn't placed against that stone, which is what we first thought . . . she crawled there.'

'What does that mean?'

'It means even after the head injury she sustained, she was still alive when her body was dumped.'

Alive?

My sister was conscious when she died, bleeding from her head, all alone in the cold?

I feel hot. It's so hot in here. I'm burning up. I take off my jumper and scarf, and push the hot coffee mug away, the contents spilling out more on the table. 'Sorry, I'll clean that.'

I rush to the sink and find a cloth by the taps. Soaking it in warm water, I hurry back and start wiping the table.

Birkens rises to his feet and gently places a hand on my shoulder. 'Alex, it's fine, leave it.'

'I need to clean it. I made a mess. I . . . I . . .' The cloth drops by my feet, and my body collapses into the chair behind me.

'She could have survived it. If someone had come along and seen her, she could be alive today?'

'We don't know that for sure. It was a pretty substantial blow to the head. She may not have survived even if she had been found in time.'

'But she could have. And that chance – that small chance – is enough.' I bow my head and clasp my hands behind my neck. 'Detective?'

'Yes?'

'I want to kill this guy.'

'Me too.'

Chapter Twenty: 17.01.2016

I can hear the birds from my window when I wake. They crow and squawk. Birds are sometimes all I see in the sky. Seagulls, crows, blackbirds. They dance among the clouds.

Every time I close my eyes, I see Olivia. Every time I open my eyes, I see her.

She's everywhere here. Her ballet shoes sit in the hallway. Her mascara is by the sink. Even the birds outside remind me of her.

I didn't think it was possible to miss a person so much that it physically hurts. My tummy aches, my eyes sting, my limbs are heavy and fight against movement. I've been in bed since Friday. I didn't get up yesterday at all. I just couldn't. Sleep came when it could, but its relief was sparse and sometimes punishing. Nightmares of Olivia crawling for her life across the grass haunted me. Her fingertips crawling for something, for someone.

Did she know she was dying? Was she looking at the sky above trying to find the birds in the darkness? Did they dance for her? Or did they forsake her, like we all did?

I push my face into my pillow harder to stop myself from crying out.

Why did Birkens have to tell me that? I was so blissfully ignorant in how she died. And now, I see her desperation, her fear, and maybe even for a few moments, her hope.

A gentle knock at my door shakes me from my own thoughts. I don't answer. I want to be left alone. I can try to sleep off another day of my life.

'Alex? It's the phone.'

It'll be Siobhan. She's been calling me constantly since the funeral. I've barely talked to her. Not that I'm up for much conversation now.

'It's the detective.'

The covers slide off me as I rise from the bed. I can tell my dad is shocked to see my appearance when I swing open the door.

'Which phone?' I mutter.

'The one in the kitchen.'

He follows me down the stairs but not into the kitchen. I don't know where he goes, but he disappears often now. He's shrinking fast. Soon he'll be nothing. Like my sister.

I cradle the phone in my hands, and speak carefully. 'Hello?'

'Alex, it's Detective Inspector Birkens.'

I don't say anything.

'Can you come to the station today?'

'It's a Sunday. Why?'

'I need to ask you some more questions.'

'OK.' I hang up the phone. I don't want to go to the station today, but I'll answer his questions.

I change quickly. I don't even shower. No need. I'll be right back in bed by this afternoon. I grab my raincoat and slide into my boots, and make my way onto the main road to Birkens' cottage. I know a shortcut now – over the wire fence at the dairy farm and through their field.

The rain is more of a mist now, dense and heavy like a wet blanket. The rain settles into my hair and on the collar of my coat. It feels refreshing actually. I don't even feel the cold any more. My body is numb, and void of any desires of warmth and comfort.

When I reach Birkens' home, the chimney is surrounded by a dark cloud and I know he's still burning his fire and hasn't left for the station yet.

I knock three times and wipe the rain from my face with the back of my hand.

He answers and looks surprised. 'Alex, I said down at the station.' He doesn't even invite me in.

'I don't want to go to the station today. Too many people. I just want to sit here for a while, answer your questions and go back to bed again. Can you put the kettle on?'

He fumbles around for a response then finally shrugs and opens the door wider. 'OK, fine.'

The entryway is a mess. His wellies are against the wall and caked in mud. Newspapers and mail pile up

blames herself. She probably thinks the police
oo.'

re looking at this boyfriend as our priority sus-

alk to her,' I say, rising from my chair. I put my
ck on and start for the door.

know, Alex . . . it would be normal in this kind
tion to not be OK with anything.'

t do you mean?'

an, you don't always have to be so strong, so

n the door, letting the chilly January wind into
se. 'Yes I do,' I say as I step over the edge and
oor slam behind me.

on the oval-shaped table. Cardboard boxes of file folders and papers are stacked up high beside each other.
There's even an old coffee mug on top of a folder that
sits on the table beside the mail and his keys.

He takes me back into the kitchen and flips the kettle
on. 'Coffee?'

I nod my head.

His armchair is filled with newspapers, so I sit in the chair
opposite. The kettle churns and boils behind me, the bubbling
getting louder. 'Did you find anything on the boyfriend?'

'What?' he shouts over the kettle.

'Do you know anything more about the boyfriend?'
I say again, louder, my voice competing with the whistling of the kettle.

Birkens turns the switch and pulls it off the base,
letting it cool down. 'Sorry,' he mutters, as a splash of
hot water hits his fingers. He swears loudly then quickly
looks at me.

I shrug and sit back down in the chair.

He pours two mugs of strong black coffee, and stirs
milk into one. He leans over to hand me mine. His hand
trembles slightly and his thumb is already getting red
from the hot water. 'Now, what did you say?'

'The boyfriend?'

He rubs his forehead, 'No, nothing yet.'

Clasping the mug in my hands, I sink a little lower
into the chair.

'That's actually why I wanted to talk to you today. I

need you to talk to Emily Morrison again. We need to find out more about this boyfriend.'

'I don't think she knows anything else.'

'She must. Even a small detail can be big in this investigation.'

'OK,' I say, glancing up at the framed photo of his son.

We sit in silence for a while. A thin skin forms on the top of the coffee mug and steam no longer rises from it.

'Are you back in school yet?' he asks, finally breaking the blanket of silence that's formed between us.

'No, not yet.'

'Why not?'

I shrug. I don't know what to say. I don't want to go back because I think it's pointless. School, friends, homework. It all seems so trivial now, so mundane. Life is so short, and so temperamental. Your life could end at any time, any moment, and you'll have spent it taking the bus to and from school, gossiping about the cute boy that delivers your Sunday morning newspaper, eating soggy sandwiches in the lunch room with people who probably won't be your friends in five years' time. Why would I do all that, knowing what I do? That at the end of the day, our lives are so . . . meaningless.

Olivia had ambition, she had dreams, a future. And that was taken from her, ripped from her, in a moment. And while she dragged her broken body across the mud, probably begging for her life, someone stood over her thinking exactly what I am now – life is worthless.

Her life certainly was to someon
her life was easy.

'How do you feel after what
night?' he asks.

'I need to know everything,
I need to know.'

He nods, and watches me sl
full coffee mug down on the ta
tired of holding it, tired of pret

'I called your parents this m
we got the biological test result
we took –'

'The what?'

'DNA testing.' He shifts in
empty mug down beside mi
found in the car – type B, whi
unknown hair follicles. The la
nostics and the results don't m
in our current database on tho
offended –'

'Even –'

'Even Mr Sheffield. I ran hi
There was someone in the car
took her body – post fatal blo
her to the Stones. But we d
why it's really important tha
tried. I called round at her h
and she acted like she had
new boyfriend.'

Her life certainly was to someone. To someone, ending her life was easy.

'How do you feel after what I told you the other night?' he asks.

'I need to know everything, as hard as it might be. I need to know.'

He nods, and watches me slowly as I place the still full coffee mug down on the table in front of me. I'm tired of holding it, tired of pretending to drink it.

'I called your parents this morning and told them, we got the biological test results from the car samples we took –'

'The what?'

'DNA testing.' He shifts in the chair and puts his empty mug down beside mine. 'There was blood found in the car – type B, which is Olivia's, and some unknown hair follicles. The lab in Aberdeen ran diagnostics and the results don't match anything we have in our current database on those who have previously offended –'

'Even –'

'Even Mr Sheffield. I ran his myself. It's not a match. There was someone in the car with her, someone who took her body – post fatal blow – into the car to drive her to the Stones. But we don't know who. This is why it's really important that you talk to Emily. I've tried. I called round at her house yesterday morning and she acted like she had no idea that Olivia had a new boyfriend.'

'She blames herself. She probably thinks the police might too.'

'We're looking at this boyfriend as our priority suspect.'

'I'll talk to her,' I say, rising from my chair. I put my coat back on and start for the door.

'You know, Alex . . . it would be normal in this kind of situation to not be OK with anything.'

'What do you mean?'

'I mean, you don't always have to be so strong, so brave.'

I open the door, letting the chilly January wind into the house. 'Yes I do,' I say as I step over the edge and let the door slam behind me.

on the oval-shaped table. Cardboard boxes of file folders and papers are stacked up high beside each other. There's even an old coffee mug on top of a folder that sits on the table beside the mail and his keys.

He takes me back into the kitchen and flips the kettle on. 'Coffee?'

I nod my head.

His armchair is filled with newspapers, so I sit in the chair opposite. The kettle churns and boils behind me, the bubbling getting louder. 'Did you find anything on the boyfriend?'

'What?' he shouts over the kettle.

'Do you know anything more about the boyfriend?' I say again, louder, my voice competing with the whistling of the kettle.

Birkens turns the switch and pulls it off the base, letting it cool down. 'Sorry,' he mutters, as a splash of hot water hits his fingers. He swears loudly then quickly looks at me.

I shrug and sit back down in the chair.

He pours two mugs of strong black coffee, and stirs milk into one. He leans over to hand me mine. His hand trembles slightly and his thumb is already getting red from the hot water. 'Now, what did you say?'

'The boyfriend?'

He rubs his forehead, 'No, nothing yet.'

Clasping the mug in my hands, I sink a little lower into the chair.

'That's actually why I wanted to talk to you today. I

need you to talk to Emily Morrison again. We need to find out more about this boyfriend.'

'I don't think she knows anything else.'

'She must. Even a small detail can be big in this investigation.'

'OK,' I say, glancing up at the framed photo of his son.

We sit in silence for a while. A thin skin forms on the top of the coffee mug and steam no longer rises from it.

'Are you back in school yet?' he asks, finally breaking the blanket of silence that's formed between us.

'No, not yet.'

'Why not?'

I shrug. I don't know what to say. I don't want to go back because I think it's pointless. School, friends, homework. It all seems so trivial now, so mundane. Life is so short, and so temperamental. Your life could end at any time, any moment, and you'll have spent it taking the bus to and from school, gossiping about the cute boy that delivers your Sunday morning newspaper, eating soggy sandwiches in the lunch room with people who probably won't be your friends in five years' time. Why would I do all that, knowing what I do? That at the end of the day, our lives are so . . . meaningless.

Olivia had ambition, she had dreams, a future. And that was taken from her, ripped from her, in a moment. And while she dragged her broken body across the mud, probably begging for her life, someone stood over her thinking exactly what I am now – life is worthless.

Chapter Twenty-One: 19.01.2016

I wait for Emily outside school at 3.20 p.m.

I stand near the pale blue sign, early yellow daffodils poking their way out of the frosty ground. Above me, two girls hang out of the window and gaze down at the steady stream of cars moving into the car park. I wonder if they know who I am, maybe why I stand here, waiting.

The familiar bell rings and students pour out of the double doors, some in their navy uniforms, others in jeans and jumpers for Casual Friday. A couple of teachers sneak out the side exit carrying their coats and hats and rush to their cars before the headmistress comes out. Eager to get home, one drops her scarf.

The thick yellow fabric billows slightly in the wind, and falls slowly towards the icy floor. When it lands, it stretches wide, reminding me of the yellow daffodils pushing their way up from winter's tight grasp.

I lightly jog over and scoop it up off the ground. 'Excuse me,' I call after her.

She turns around and immediately tenses around the shoulders.

'Oh, hi Miss Campbell. I didn't recognize you there,' I mumble.

She looks anxious to see me. I thought we had had a nice connection in Art. She always encouraged me to bring in my dried flowers for life drawing assignments. She enjoyed my calluna display, said the lavender hues popped against the grey backboard I chose.

I had signed up for this year's art field trip to Windermere in the Lake District but I don't think I'll be going to that. I hope Mum and Dad get their deposit back. Olivia had even talked about going with me. She was going to ask if she could combine her end-of-year field trip with mine. She was going to finish her English thesis on William Wordsworth while I roamed the brooks and valleys looking for lady's bedstraw and cowslips. My field trip assignment would focus on Cumbrian wildflowers.

I wonder if I'll get a Fail for not submitting it. It's still four months away, but I can't imagine being ready to come back to school, being ready to face my friends and teachers. Miss Campbell was a great example of that; she can barely look me in the eye. Why does tragedy make people so uncomfortable?

'Alexandra,' she says walking closer to me, 'I didn't know you were back at school?'

'I'm not. I'm just waiting for someone.'

'Oh,' she says, fidgeting with her car keys. I can tell she wants to turn and run. 'I'm really sorry about your sister. I never had her in my class but I knew she was a good student. I heard she was going to London to dance.'

I nod. *Not any more*, I want to say. But I don't. I wouldn't want to hear those words spoken out loud, and I know Miss Campbell wouldn't want to hear them either. She already looks uncomfortable enough.

'And you, how are you?' she finally says. Her fingers grip the yellow scarf. Part of it dangles down to her knees, and I worry she might drop it again.

'I'm fine,' I lie.

'Will you be back soon?'

'I'm not sure yet. We're still waiting to . . .' To what – catch her killer? The words now sound ridiculous to me. I'm really going to help the detective inspector find the person who murdered my sister? Me, a sixteen-year-old?

Her keys slip between her middle fingers. She wants to go. She doesn't know what else to say to me, and I don't know how to respond to her questions.

'Well, I'd better get going,' I say, allowing Miss Campbell some relief. 'Bye.'

'Goodbye. Please send my condolences to your parents,' she calls after me as I start to walk away.

This is exactly why I'm not ready to come back to school to face people.

'Alex!'

I look up and see Andy jogging towards me.

Great.

He slows his jog and comes to a stop in front of me,

taking me in. For a moment I think he looks relieved to see me. 'Are you here to see me?'

Oh.

'Um no, actually I'm here to see Olivia's friend, Emily.'

He snorts quietly then looks up at the sky. The sun is already setting. Swirls of pale corals and reds sneak up on a thick blanket of grey. I can hear the seagulls near the beach. You can even see the coastline from some of the classrooms on the top floor.

He looks back at me and suddenly a vacuum of emptiness seems to have formed between us. I don't know how to be normal any more. So much has changed between us. We once shared the same taste in music and films, and laughed at the same jokes. But now, I don't listen to music. I don't watch films. And I don't want to laugh.

'So, that's it, huh?'

'What?' I shrug.

'You used to never stop talking.'

'I don't have much to say these days,' I say, glancing over his shoulder for Emily.

'Are you coming back to school soon?'

'I don't know.'

'Me and Siobhan miss you.'

'Me and Siobhan?' Since when did the two of them become a 'we'?

I don't know what to say to that. Siobhan and I were best friends long before we met Andy. I had a crush on him so we started spending more time together. We all got along so well. But it was always 'the three of us', or at least 'me and Andy'. Not 'Siobhan and Andy'. I really have missed a lot not being here.

'What do you do all day long?' he asks.

'I meet with the detective on Olivia's case, I help out around the house. Mum's not been doing well –'

'I wouldn't know. You don't return my calls. Or Siobhan's.'

Why does he keep bringing her up?

'There's nothing to tell. My sister was murdered. You pretty much know exactly what I do. Sorry it's not more exciting for you.'

'That's not what I –'

'Andy, I have to go. I see Emily.' I pass him and feel his eyes on me as I jog away. What does he want me to say? He can't expect me to just pick up where I left off before Olivia died. I'm not the same person. And I don't have time for friends.

I see her red hair bobbing up and down, off her shoulders. She's wearing a dark navy coat which makes the colour of her hair burst against it. She doesn't notice me so I hurry after her. She merges into a group of people, and now I can't see her.

Pushing into the group, I snake around people as they shuffle around greeting each other and making plans for the weekend. The sounds of school buses pulling out startles me and I spin around to see Emily standing there, looking at me.

She looks pale, ashen like a ghost. Her mouth is agape for a moment then she comes to, and touches my arm gently. 'Alex, sorry. I . . .' She smiles but looks uncomfortable. Her hand trembles as she tucks a loose strand of hair behind her ear. 'You just look so much like Olivia. I hadn't realized how much until just now.'

No one had really compared me to my sister before. I always thought we were so different from each other.

'I didn't mean to just show up like this, but I wanted to talk. Do you have any time?'

'Now?'

'I can walk back with you?'

She starts to walk away from the crowd, the noise, the triviality of everyday life. She glances back and waits for me to follow. 'Are you coming?'

We walk up towards Cairston Road and head towards the ferry terminal. The crimson sky flutters above us, and the seagulls' caterwauling gets louder as we pass the old Fisherman's Society, near where they built a brand new squash club that towers above the other commercial buildings and residences.

Siobhan and I used to walk down to the beach sometimes after school. We'd meet at the side exit, by the Physics wing, and walk down Ferry Road. We'd talk about our day, laugh about what happened in P.E that morning, make plans for Saturday night, which usually consisted of Siobhan's house, whatever alcohol she could steal from her parents without them detecting it, and *The X Factor*. Occasionally we'd strut into one of the pubs in town, feigning confidence, and promptly be asked to show identification. Siobhan looked like she could be eighteen, but me, I always got us in trouble. I barely passed for my own age, let alone someone who's older.

When Siobhan and I finally got to the shoreline, we'd watch the sun go down, the intensity of the colours simmering until a golden shimmer peppered the sky before finally caving to darkness. I invited Andy along a few times. He said he'd never really seen a sunset from start to finish. I wouldn't watch it any other way.

We'd hear the children come out of primary school. The guileless chattering of children seemed so innocent at the time, so funny to us. But now, I missed it. I craved the naivety, the protection of childhood. The unaffected, starry-eyed wonder of children, those who'd never experienced loss before. Those who would never face tragedy. I was not one of them, not now.

'I'm sorry about the other night, at the memorial,' Emily finally says, looking right before she crosses the road.

I hurry after her. 'That's actually what I wanted to talk to you about.' We cross the roundabout and start up Hillside Road, the coastline at our backs.

'Did Olivia say anything else to you about her new boyfriend?'

'I told you everything I know.'

'You said you didn't know his name?'

'Yes, or his age.'

'Do you know if he went to Stromness Academy or Kirkwall Grammar?'

'She said I wouldn't know him when I asked his name, so he must go to Kirkwall Grammar?'

'So, Kirkwall Grammar, maybe S6?'

'Maybe. I don't know if he'd left school already.'

Taking a left on Cauldhame Road, the sun sets behind us and the grey sky looms overhead, the moon pushing through a cluster of clouds.

We're close to her house.

I need more information.

I stop walking and turn to her. 'Emily, I need to know everything you know. The police are investigating this. He – whoever "he" is – might be a suspect, our only suspect.'

She glances behind her at her house in the distance, the warmth and security beckoning her return. 'I wish I could help you, I do. But I don't know much She was secretive about him. That's why we fought. All I know is that he drove a car, he's likely not someone who goes to Academy, and that he was part of that stupid club she did on Thursdays.'

'What club? Dance?'

'No, the sad club or something.'

'The what?'

'I better get going. My mum's already going to freak out when she knows I walked home from school. I promised her I'd take the bus.'

'Wait, tell me about this club.'

'I don't know much about it. Look, I really have to go. Sorry.'

'OK, I'll see you later then.'

'Alex, you shouldn't be out here either. Orkney's not safe until this guy is found.'

'You think it's a man too then?'

'Of course. What woman would do this?'

'You're right,' I scoff. 'Thanks, Emily.'

She smiles and starts jogging lightly down the road, not looking back. It's then I realize, we don't know who the killer is. It could be anyone.

Even someone who was close to her.

Even a friend.

Chapter Twenty-Two: 20.01.2016

'Why do I even bother asking you to come to the station?' Birkens is standing in his doorway, coat over his arm.

'I don't know, but maybe you should stop,' I say, pushing past him. I go into the kitchen, the path very familiar to me now, and flip the kettle on.

Sighing, he follows me into the kitchen and flings his coat over the cabinet. 'Coffee then. No milk.'

'Did you find out anything on the "sad club"?' I shout over the seething and roiling of the kettle.

He disappears into another room and returns with a large folder file in hand. Knocking into the cabinet, he sends his coat to the floor. The small Superman chain rolls onto the tiled kitchen flooring. I rush over and scoop it up before he sees it. Picking up his coat, I slide it into the left pocket and position it back on the cabinet, with the longer end stretching down towards the floor.

The kettle finally stops roaring, and Birkens pats the chair in front of him, motioning me to join him at the table.

'Well?' I ask, settling into the armchair in front of him.

'Where's my coffee?' he asks, putting the folder down on his lap.

Rolling my eyes, I prepare two mugs of coffee at the sink. One with a splash of milk, both with a quick stir of a teaspoon.

I hand one to him, and rest the other one on the table knowing I won't touch it.

He starts taking apart the folder, separating papers and photos. 'S.A.D. not "sad" – Schools Against Drugs. It's an organization, or club of some kind. Meets on Thursdays at the community centre.'

'Olivia was a part of that?'

'Looks like she joined in September.'

'Why?'

'Apparently it looks good on the CV.'

'So do you think she met her boyfriend here?'

He takes a quick swig of coffee and croaks. 'Hot!' He splutters for a moment then pulls out a 7x5 photo and hands it to me. It's of a group of teenagers. Olivia stands in the middle, between two other female students. One I recognize from her year, Kirsty something. But I didn't recognize the others.

He pulls out a printed piece of paper and starts reading down the list: 'Kirsty Maclean – in your sister's year at Stromness Academy, they knew each other but weren't really friends; Jennifer MacIntyre – goes to Kirkwall Grammar –'

He looks at the coffee mug still sitting on the table beside me. 'Aren't you going to drink that?' he asks.

I slide the mug closer to me but don't lift it.

'Cheryl Black – in the year below Olivia –'

'I know Cheryl. Her brother died of an overdose three years ago. It was in the newspaper.'

'Yeah, in 2013. He was nineteen.'

A tall boy with sandy brown hair stands behind my sister, his teeth gleaming as he smiles awkwardly. He's wearing a grey hooded zip-up with a blue shirt collar sticking out. He's handsome, his face familiar. 'Who's that?'

'Nick Murray. Also goes to Kirkwall Grammar. We're looking into him.'

'Looks a little like James,' I say, brushing my thumb over his face.

Who are you?

'The boy on the left is Stuart Wilmot, also goes to Kirkwall Grammar –'

'Looking into him too?'

Birkens shakes his head and tips the rest of his coffee mug back, taking in every last drop. He shakes his head, and places the mug back down beside my full one. 'Not him.'

'Why not?'

'Because he was on holiday in Majorca between the 26th of December and the 3rd of January.'

I lean back in the armchair and cross my arms. 'So, what now?'

'We still have skin cells and hair follicles from your sister's car that we need to match to someone. We need to start testing everyone who was at the party and everyone who had the opportunity to get close to Olivia on the night of the 31st. She might have known her killer.'

'So do that.'

'Alex, I need DNA samples from you and your parents.'

'Oh. You think we had something to do with Olivia's murder?' My stomach churns, and I feel my cheeks getting hot.

'No, of course not. But your fingerprints and hair and skin cells will be all over the car, as will your parents', the investigating police including me, and likely Emily and James. I need to start ruling out people so we can narrow the list down to persons of interest. It's protocol, that's all.'

'OK, I'm ready.'

'Not here. You're actually going to have to go to the station for this one. I don't have DNA kits here.'

'Will it hurt?'

He waves his hand. 'Nah. A saliva swab, a few strands of hair. It's nothing. They'll take mine too, and everyone else on the investigation team since we've been all over that car since it was brought in. We need to eliminate ourselves so we're not chasing false leads.'

I intertwine my fingers and press them tightly shut. I don't know why, but I'm nervous about this test.

He leans in and catches my eye. 'How about we go in tomorrow and get it done together?'

'OK. Thank you.'

The sky is overcast today. Fog sits on the rooftops and cliff edges of Stromness. In a fortnight, people would gather at the standing stones near where my sister was found. Not because of her, but because of the Imbolc ceremony. Neighbours and friends say goodbye to winter and symbolize the coming of spring with music, poetry, honey cake, and ale. But I'm not ready to say goodbye yet. There's still so much to do, so much to say.

I won't be ready to welcome spring, or any new changes, until we know who killed my sister. And why.

I reach the cemetery in the early afternoon, when the sun should be highest in the sky. The fog has thickened, layering the icy air in a dense blanket. Rows of standing stones, much like the one Olivia died at, line the graves, each with a different name. So many gravestones for such a small island.

I start at the back row, my feet moving along each row. Names. Dates. Brief messages from loved ones. Some have flowers at the base of the stone. Others have none. Some stones are grey, some are beige, some are made of marble while others have a little limestone swirled in that makes them stand out. I don't know what my parents chose for Olivia's.

I loop up to the next row, then the next. This row is

shorter than the rest, the graves not yet filled. Olivia's must be here.

I don't have to walk far until I see it. Marble, with a shimmer of black throughout. A small slate plaque underneath too – *Olivia Maria McCarthey, 18 years old, born 8 October 1998. Beloved daughter, sister, and friend. You will forever be in our hearts.*

A handful of purple wildflowers sit in a pale blue vase next to the slate plaque, which has a quote about life being a dance. A few white rose petals are scattered over the plaque and around the headstone. A small piece of lined paper, folded up many times, sits beside the blue vase.

It's not my letter to read, my note to feel, but I open it. Inside are two words, simple but burdened with the stench of guilt and remorse – I'm sorry.

Chapter Twenty-Three: 21.01.2016

'And you found this at the cemetery beside her grave-stone?'

We stand in Birkens' kitchen. He holds the note in his hand and a steaming hot mug in the other.

'What makes you think it's written for Olivia?'

'Who else would say something like that? "I'm sorry"? Sorry for what? For killing her accidentally? For shoving her body somewhere then dumping her a few days later half-alive? It's a message. I'm sure it is.'

He reads it again. 'It can't be a coincidence.'

'Now we're on the same page!'

'I'm going to need handwriting samples from every-one on the list, including from you and your parents, to eliminate people.'

'Great, let's do it now.'

He gets me a blue pen and a small note from the drawer under the shelves where he keeps the photo of his son. He puts his mug down and places the paper in front of me.

'What should I write?'

'Exactly that – "I'm sorry." You've seen it now.

Typically when I ask for a handwriting sample, I don't tend to show the person the writing in question.'

'I think we're both pretty certain I'm not the killer.' The pen quivers in my hand slightly, and I don't know why. Perhaps the two words are something that I have wanted to say to my sister since this started. I'm sorry for not waiting up for you, I'm sorry for being mad at you for standing me up that night, I'm sorry for thinking you were just staying at a friend's house and had forgotten to call, I'm sorry for being too busy for you over the years. I'm sorry for growing up, if that meant growing apart. And most of all, I'm so sorry that this happened to you, and that you died alone and scared.

'What's wrong?' he asks.

'Nothing,' I mutter, as I start writing on the paper.

I'm.

Sorry.

I hand the pen and the paper back to him, and watch as he files it. 'Will you take samples from my parents?'

'Yes, and from Olivia's friends, and those who really knew her. I'll go round to James's later and take his too.'

'He'll be at school until 3.20.'

'Not him. Sounds like he also decided to take some time off school after Olivia's death. He hasn't been back since her body was found.'

'Really? He acted like he didn't care when he thought she was missing?'

'Missing is very different from dead,' says Birkens as he throws on his coat.

'Where are you going?'

'We're going to complete the bio test kits. I said I would go with you, and I will. But it needs to be done today. Ready?'

I nod my head and slide my coat on, and finally my hat.

As the car passes the ocean, seagulls flying high overhead, I can't help but think about James. I didn't realise how much he was hurting. Olivia cared about him deeply, I think. All that time I thought it was him that made her unhappy, but if I think back before this secret boyfriend, Olivia was truly happy with him. It was after him, that she wasn't. Perhaps he never stopped loving her. It's hard not to love her. She drew people to her. She was a magnet for attention, for admiration. She was everything I wasn't.

The car slows to a stop and Birkens parks in between two white lines and in front of a reserved parking sign. If we drove a little further up that road, I'd see the Ring of Brodgar where Olivia's body was found. I'd see the beginning of all of this. And the end for many other things.

I follow Birkens into the station, sign in, again the pen quivering between my fingers. We go into the family interview room and wait for the technician.

The technician is a woman. Long red hair, little too much plum lipstick on. I watch as Birkens goes through the kit. He sits half on the edge of the table, half standing as she sticks a cotton swab in his mouth and brushes the inside of his cheek. Then she pulls out a strand or two of hair and slides them inside a plastic test tube. Lastly, she puts her hand over his, rolls his index finger and thumb in black ink on a rectangular pad and rolls them again on a sheet of paper.

She gives him a wet wipe to remove the ink, changes her gloves, then waits for me to walk closer to the table.

'It doesn't hurt,' says Birkens as he shifts to the other side of the table.

My feet shuffle closer until the cold metal edge of the table hits my hip. The woman steps closer and touches my face. The rubber of her glove feels weird, it reminds me of going to the dentist. And just like the dentist, she asks me to open my mouth wide.

The cotton sticks to the inside of my cheek and moves upward. It doesn't hurt, like Birkens said, but it feels rough. My scalp pinches as she takes my hair, and she presses my fingers down into the ink hard, the tips whitening under the pressure.

And just like that, my entire biological make-up is extracted from me. After, Birkens walks me to the door.

'And my parents?'

'They've already been in.' He holds the station door slightly open for me to take from him. 'You OK?'

'Yeah,' I say quietly.

'Straight home,' he adds.

'Of course.' I take the door from him and slip out, hearing it swing shut behind me. But I don't go straight home. I start walking towards Ireland Road. Where James lives.

The sun is already setting behind me. Scatterings of red hues and purple tints patched into the sky like a quilt. After about twenty-five minutes, the sun is low in the sky, only a sliver of coral left behind. It's quiet this evening. No cars pass me, but I hear them in the distance. People will be returning home from work soon, exhausted after a long day, most have been sat at a computer for hours and hours.

I wonder if my dad missed his work. Perhaps he would have welcomed the distraction, the opportunity to fill his head with thoughts other than Olivia. I know school might be that for me, but I'm just not ready. Not yet.

I count the houses, each blending into the next, until I find his. I spent a lot of time here once. James, Olivia and I would watch movies together, play Monopoly or Hotel. Sometimes Emily would come over, and her and my sister would giggle together and tease James.

He was always nice to me. He treated me like a sister too, made me feel part of the family that he, Olivia and Emily had built together. He made me want that for myself, and I thought I had found that with Siobhan and Andy. But then everything changed, and now I just don't know anything any more.

Olivia would have wanted me to check in on him. She would have wanted him to be OK.

When I reach his house, his lights are on. The

driveway is empty but I can hear the TV playing from inside. It's loud, and disrupts an otherwise silent road.

I ring the bell, once, twice. After the third time, the TV sound goes down and a tall silhouette fills the glass door. It opens and James is standing there. He looks shocked. He's pale, ashen. He staggers back and grips the doorframe with his hand. 'Olivia?' he stutters. His hair is dishevelled and his eyes are blurred.

'No, James. It's me. Alex.'

He rubs his face and for a split second I think he's about to cry. He takes a deep breath. 'Sorry, you just looked so much like . . .'

He steps back and lets me come inside. The living room is a mess. Empty lager cans lie on the carpet by the sofa, some scrunched, others still upright and standing. The air that enters with me is fresh and chilled from the outside, and tries to fill the space to freshen it. But it's warm in here, and the smell of stale alcohol lingers thick in the air.

'Where's your mum?'

He collapses on the sofa. 'She's doing the evening shift at the hospital. She won't be back until after midnight.'

I sit beside him, keeping a little distance. 'Sorry to just stop by like this, but I wanted to see how you were doing.'

'Shouldn't I be asking you that?'

'You lost her too,' I say quietly.

His face contorts a little, then he gets up quickly and

disappears into the kitchen. He takes a few moments to return but when he does he has another can of lager in his hand. He slides it into mine, then sits down again beside me. 'I just thought she was staying at Emily's or this new boyfriend's. I never imagined . . . she'd never come back.'

'Me neither.'

He leans over and puts his hand on his face. His sounds are muffled but I think he's trying to use words. He scoots back, and looks at me. I turn away but I can feel his eyes still on me, watching my every move. This feels strange, wrong. Why is he looking at me like that?

I shift uncomfortably on the sofa as he moves closer to me. I hold the can between both hands, feeling the coldness on my skin. He moves even closer to me, and I squeeze the can even tighter. I grit my teeth, as he reaches a hand towards my face and brushes a strand of my hair off my cheek.

'You look so much like her,' he whispers to me, his breath smelling of alcohol. Every cell in my body screams for me to get up and run, but now he has his arm around me so tight. Too tight. I can't breathe, air chokes in my lungs.

'I have to go,' I stammer, trying to get up from the sofa. He gently pushes me back down.

'No, stay. I don't want to be alone.'

I feel his warm breath on my skin as he nuzzles into my hair. My stomach churns. I push him off. 'Get off of me!' I yell, struggling up from the sofa. The can drops on the floor and frothy amber liquid spills out onto the carpet.

He looks at me, his eyes big and wide. 'I'm so sorry. I don't know what got into me.' Tears start rolling down his cheeks. He reaches up a hand to me, begging me to stay. 'You just remind me so much of her. I miss her so much.'

'I do too, but I'm not her. I'm not her!' I cry out, the anger and frustration bubbling inside me. I grab my bag from the floor and run for the door. But he's fast, and he gets up and puts his hand on my shoulder.

'Wait . . .' he pleads.

But I don't stop, I heave open the door and run out into the night. The cool air whips at my face as I jog all the way. I want to scream into the night. I want to scream her name over and over and over. I want her to hear it. I suddenly feel like the air has been sucked out of me. I feel like someone is suffocating me, not letting go, like I am back at his house, feeling his foul breath on my skin. I have to get rid of that memory. I need to remember the past, before everything changed, when he made me hot chocolate and let me win at Monopoly. Not this moment. I don't want to remember this James. Why does everything have to change? Why does everything have to get ruined?

I fling open the front door, and run up the stairs. I slam the bathroom door shut, and take off my clothes. I turn on the shower, and jump in before it has even warmed up. The icy water runs down my back and through my hair. I scrub at my skin, furiously trying to wipe away the night. By the time the water has heated up, my skin is red raw and numb.

I climb out and wrap a towel around me. I crouch and open the cabinet underneath the sink, looking for my hairbrush. The cabinet is a mess. As I unload the shampoos, soaps, and shaving creams onto the floor, I find a box of dye. The woman on the front has short dark hair, and is smiling. I grab a pair of scissors from my dad's shaving kit and stand up.

I look in the mirror at my long hair, still wet from the shower. He was right, I do look like her. I can't look at myself. My hand trembles as I hold the scissors close to me. I feel them grip onto a chunk of my hair and watch as the wet strands flop down to the ground. Then I keep cutting. The more I cut, the less I look like her. Hair falls down my shoulders, trickles down my back, climbs down my legs. And when I finish, I stand there, shivering and naked, standing on a blanket of hair as soft as feathers on a bird.

Chapter Twenty-Four: 22.01.2016

The sky glistens through the small kitchen window, an array of coppery reds and amber hues stretching wide across the light wood flooring around my feet. I can hear sheep in the background, a rooster a little further back, and then eventually the rustling of Birkens' papers beside me. His house sits on the bay, not too far from the police station, beyond a maze of winding single-lane roads and dipping valleys. I wonder if he likes it here, if it's peaceful, if he feels at home, if he feels safe. I don't know what that feels like any more, to feel safe. My hands start to tremble every time I walk out my front door. Sweat forms on the back of my neck, even though my body feels ice cold, and my palms get clammy. And for a moment I look back, and contemplate turning around. This isn't normal. This can't be normal. But then again, what is, now?

I tug at my hair, the short strands feeling unfamiliar and new to me. I probably shouldn't have been so rash. A coldness creeps up my spine, making me shiver.

'Nice haircut, by the way,' he says, not even looking up over his file.

I hold the coffee mug tighter in my hands, the steam rising and disappearing in the air above it. I haven't touched a drop. I never touch a drop. I don't like coffee, yet every morning when I knock on his door, he asks me if I want one and I always say yes. I don't even know why he lets me in. I don't know why I come. But I do. I get up, brush my teeth, pull on some old jeans and slide into my sister's brown leather walking boots and start walking. I never think about where I'm going, I just walk. And yet I always end up here, at this door, in this house, holding yet another cup of unappealing coffee in my hands. I put the mug down on the table and look at him. His eyebrows furrow as his eyes skim the lines on the page. He looks like my dad when he reads the newspaper, or another article about my sister. Not much else to write about here.

He stops and lowers the file folder, taking me in. 'You shouldn't be here so much.'

'Why not?'

'It's not right. People are talking.'

'What are they saying?'

'They're saying...' He drops the folder on the table, the cardboard slapping against the wood. 'Look, you shouldn't be around all this so much.'

'Around what? The murder?' I laugh. Then all of a sudden, it doesn't seem so funny. It seems . . . wrong. 'Too late. It's around *me*.'

I slide off the chair and walk over to the window, taking in the sunrise. 'Why don't you move home after this? You don't have to stay here. You could work for Edinburgh police again.'

'I don't want to talk about my personal life.'

'Didn't stop you the other day.'

The air suddenly gets sharp around us and I turn to see him sitting there, his coffee mug quivering in his hands. 'Sorry,' I say quietly, and turn back to the window. I hear him get up from his chair. He walks over to the tall coat rack in the corner by the back door, and tugs his khaki green rain jacket from one of the hooks. He roughly shoves his arm into the sleeve before turning to the next one.

'You're leaving?'

'Yeah, and so are you,' he says, pulling out his car keys.

'But I've not finished my coffee.' I look down, the brown liquid no longer steaming.

He reaches over and takes the mug from my hands. 'You never do.' He places the mug in the middle of the sink next to his empty one then walks back over to the door. He opens it wide, letting a cold misty chill inside. 'Come on. I'll drop you at school.'

'I'm not in school any more, I told you.'

'No, your headmaster told your mum and dad you could take as much time off as you need. And I'm telling you, you've had enough time off. Now come on, jump in the front.'

'No.' I lean against the wall, snaking my hands behind my back.

'OK, then I'll make a personal call to the head-mistress and let her know that the police are recom-mending that Alexandra McCarthey return to school asap and that all future absences be taken seriously.'

'This is ridiculous. I don't need to be there!'

'Yes you do. And I need you to as well –'

'No, I –'

'Look, neither of us are going to find the person that killed your sister sitting here in this cottage drinking cold coffee. I can't look over these case files again. I need to get down to the station.'

He drops me at the front of the building. I don't get out at first. The building looks bigger than I remem-bered.

He doesn't wait for me to catch my breath, just unbuckles his seatbelt, then mine, reaches across and opens my door. The wintery air bursts in, and quickly fills the whole car, sucking out all the warmth from the heater.

OK, that's it then.

I slam my car door when I get out and march to the gates, stomping my feet slightly so he can see how miserable I am at this decision. I don't think he cares though.

When I get inside, the hallway feels strange under my shoes. Unfamiliar. Cold.

My belly churns and I feel light-headed. My hands grip the white-washed brick wall as I steady myself.

Why am I so nervous?

This is my school. I've been here before. I know the teachers, I've taken the classes, I sit next to some of these people at lunch. But this all feels so different today.

Maybe I'm not ready to come back.

This was a bad idea. I tried, and it didn't work. I tried. I did.

I hurry back down the hallway and push on the exit door. But before I can unseal it and let the cold air in to take me, I notice Birkens' car parked out front.

Is he really still here to make sure I don't leave?

My forehead touches the glass on the window and a deep breath escapes my lips. I'm stuck here.

Now I know how Olivia felt. Trapped.

I hoist my bag over my shoulder and trudge back down the hallway. I've already missed first period, so arriving now will just cause a disruption and draw undue attention on me. As if that was up for discussion anyway.

Everyone will be staring at me like a monkey at a zoo.

Why am I here?

School is such a joke to me now. We go to learn and experience new things. Well, I've learned too much for a sixteen-year-old, and I've definitely experienced too much.

My body reaches the door before my mind has caught up. Here I am. At school. My fingers tremble slightly, hovering over the doorknob.

Turn it.

But I can't. This just feels too soon, too rushed.

Maybe I can sneak out the side door by the PE hall. If Birkens is still there, he shouldn't be able to see me from that side of the building.

As I turn the leave, the door suddenly swings open. My physics teacher, Mr Cruickshank is standing in the doorway looking at me. 'Alex. I wasn't expecting you today.'

'I didn't expect to be back today,' I respond, honestly. I don't want to add that I was driven here by a detective inspector and that he's currently parked outside the building to make sure I stay.

'Well, come in. We've missed you.' He holds the door wider, gesturing me inside.

I hate this.

I hate this.

My feet shuffle through, bag awkwardly swinging by my side. The first face I see among the sea of gawking eyes is Andy's. He looks surprised to see me. Maybe more surprised than I am to be here. Or perhaps he's looking at my hair.

'You remember where your seat is?' Mr Cruickshank asks.

I nod, politely. Of course I know where it is. I've only been gone for a couple of weeks. I'm not that forgetful.

I stumble to my chair, through a swarm of bulging eyes and gaping open mouths.

Monkey. Zoo.

My bag hits my leg as I drop it down hard onto the

floor. Notepads and textbooks litter each desk. I don't have mine. I'm not prepared.

'Here, you can have mine,' says the teacher, as he hands me his book. 'We're on page 48 – Matter, Motion and Force.'

My eyes start skimming the context. Acceleration equals gain of velocity over time taken.

A piece of paper lands on my open book. I glance up and see Andy smiling at me. He wants me to open it.

I uncrumple the paper in my hand and scan the letters and words.

I'm glad you're back. I missed you. How you doing? Wanna hang at the park tonight?

He gestures towards the pencil that sits on my desk. Mr Cruickshank must have put it there. I don't reach for it. I look back and shake my head, silently mouthing, 'I can't.' He pretends to pout and then watches me to see if I smile. I don't.

So much has changed between us. I can't seem to find my way back to where we used to be. Sorry. I tried. I did. Just give me more time, I'll get there. But I don't say these words to Andy. Instead I slowly fold up his message and slide it into my bag.

'OK, we're going to finish that test from yesterday. Remember the questions have multiple responses. Colour in the bubble beside your response . . .' He stops when he gets to my desk. 'Alex, don't worry about this. You weren't here last week when we covered this content –'

'That's OK. I'll try it,' I say, reaching up and sliding out a booklet from his stack.

I start by writing my name at the top but when I open it and start reading the questions, I can't seem to focus. My eyes begin blurring, and the words on the page seem to disappear before I can read them.

The clock on the wall ticks loudly, the second hand clicking away like keys on a computer. Tick. Tick. Tick. The minute hand thuds, startling me. When I look up, I see heads down, eyes on paper. Pencils scratching away.

It's so loud.

How am I supposed to concentrate?

I close my eyes tight and open them wide. It's still so loud.

The pencil trembles slightly in my hand.

When I look at the pencil, I don't see the paper. I don't see Here. I don't see Now. I see my sister sitting at the kitchen counter, her legs dangling off the bar stool, finishing her homework with a cup of tea in her hand. Her feet swing gently, hovering off the ground. She wears a thin gold ankle bracelet on her left foot. It has a small oval pendant on it, the colour of her eyes – brown with a small amber fleck.

Her fingers are playing with the O on her necklace, which she fidgeted with often. She takes a long sip from her Winnie the Pooh mug, which I got her for her birthday years ago. The colour on Tigger's face is slightly faded from the many washes, but she uses it almost every day.

In Home Economics, two years ago, I traced a design of Winnie the Pooh from a template, coloured it in with fabric markers and sewed it on to a pink pillowcase. I stuffed it and sealed it in class, and gave it to her. I told her I had made it for her, and she told me it was the best gift she would ever receive.

It still sits on her bed now.

Olivia.

Will I ever stop missing you?

When I flicker my eyes open, I see Mr Cruickshank standing over me. All the other desks in the classroom are empty. Everyone's gone. When did that happen?

'It's OK, you can finish it another time, yeah?'

I slowly look down and see my paper's completely blank. I haven't touched any questions, finished any part of it.

'Sorry, sir,' I mumble, reaching down for my bag. He steps back and lets me rise from the chair. He watches me hurry out of the classroom. And when I glance back, I see the same look that everyone seems to be giving me. Sympathy. Pity.

Andy is waiting for me outside the classroom door.

'You took ages in there,' he laughs. 'Didn't look like you got much done?'

I walk beside him, but my steps are slow and careful. The tiles under my shoes feel different.

'When did you cut your hair?'

'Yesterday.'

'It's . . . um . . . different.'

'That's what I was going for.'

We walk side by side, the awkwardness growing.

'Are you worried about the test back there? Don't be, I'm sure you'll get a free pass now because . . .'

I stop and turn my body to face him, and wait for him to finish his sentence.

His cheeks flush, and he fidgets wildly with the strap on his bag. 'Sorry, I didn't mean . . . I'm . . . I just don't know what to say,' he stutters. He reaches for my hand, sliding his into mine. But his touch feels strange, not real, like he's pretending.

'You don't have to say anything,' I say, opening my fingers and letting his hand drop. I turn and walk away, and I don't glance back. No more sympathetic looks. No more pity.

Please.

Chapter Twenty-Five: 30.12.2015

Olivia

I see him. He follows me. Every time I turn around he's there and when he's not there, I wonder where he is. I don't know if I miss him, or if I just expect him to be there when I turn around. I'm so confused. I think he knows that and that's why he can't move on. That's why *I* can't move on.

I couldn't sleep last night. I thought I saw him outside my window when I was changing for bed. I have the same routine every night. I warm a cup of milk in the microwave, kiss my papa goodnight on the cheek and poke my sister (who is always fast asleep on his shoulder) on the nose, text my mum that I'm going to sleep if she's doing the night shift, change into my pyjamas, brush my teeth and climb into bed. I read. And when a skin forms on the top of my milk, I push it to the side with a finger and drink it all. Then I turn off the lamp and sink my head into the cool pillow.

But not tonight.

Tonight, I don't warm my milk. I don't even pour it. I avoid my dad, knowing he will see the pain in my eyes and instead gently call out 'Goodnight' on the stairs. I don't touch my sister, scared she will wake this one time and ask me what's wrong. I don't change in my bedroom, I don't change at all. I lie on bed, in my clothes, and curl up so I can hug my knees to my chest. I replay the words in my head. It's over.

It's over.

It's over.

But it's not over. He won't let it be over. He'll keep following me, keep texting me. When it was his turn to end it, I accepted it. I cried. A lot. But I accepted it. I stopped calling him, texting him. I started hanging out with James again; he was always so good to me, so kind. But he pushed his way back into my life, and I let him. I shouldn't have. I knew it was mistake. I knew it was moving too fast for me. And now that it's me that ended it, now that it's my turn, he won't let me end it.

I can't do this any more. I can't lie to the people I love. I can't lie to the people I don't know. I saw her last Thursday on my way from school. His wife. She was walking down Market Street with her son. *Their* son. He skipped along beside her as she delicately held his hand. She said something to him that I couldn't hear and he laughed. I knew they had a son together, but what I didn't know – what hurts the most – was that she seemed happy. He told me that they were unhappy and that they weren't a proper family, not any more. But what I saw wasn't unhappiness. I saw contentment.

Like there was nothing in the world that could destroy her happiness, or her family. Except me.

I knew it was stupid, but I had crossed the street towards her. I needed to see her closer. I needed to see her pain, her bitterness. But when I passed her, she looked right at me and smiled. She didn't know. The only person who had exited that marriage was him, not her. It had never been her. He lied to me.

I was so angry, I could feel my cheeks burn. I ran all the way home and texted him. I told him it was over. I told him I hated him. He rang me immediately but I ignored it. And that's when he started following me. I saw him again yesterday on my way to school. He was just sitting in the car, watching me as I walked on the pavement. He opened his car door, like he was going to say my name out loud, but then I saw Sarah Harper. He must have seen her too because he closed the door and tucked his head down so she wouldn't recognize him.

He's everywhere. I need to see him. I need to tell him in person that he needs to leave me alone. It's over. And if he can't accept it then I'll tell his wife. She'll get it, she'll understand. She'll hate me, but he'll leave me alone and that's all I want right now.

I lift my phone off the bedside table and scroll through my contacts. He's in my phone as A. My hand trembles as I reread his last message: I need to see you. Please answer my calls.

I slowly type my message, lightly tapping each icon on the touchscreen.

OK. Meet me tomorrow night.

I take a deep breath and tap Send.

A knock on my bedroom door makes me jump. If it's my dad, I can't face him right now. I tiptoe over to my door and press my ear against it. There's a knock again, but this time I know it's not my dad. The force is too light, and the silhouette under the door is too delicate. I immediately open it. My sister smiles at me and walks past me, into the room.

'What are you doing? Go to bed,' I snap. I can't see her tonight. She can't be here with me in case he responds to my text. It will be harder to lie to her.

'There's a spider in my room,' she says as she climbs up into my bed. She pulls the cover over her and wriggles down, so the quilt sits right below her shoulders.

'So ask Dad to kill it.'

'He's in the shower.'

'So wait in your room until he gets out. He'll kill it then.'

'No, it's under my bed somewhere. I'm not going back in there until it's squished in a piece of toilet paper and being flushed down the toilet.'

'Well, you can't stay in my bedroom tonight.' I glance over at my phone on the bedside table. My belly flutters and I feel nauseous as I imagine my phone beeping and Alex picking it up, seeing that text from him.

'Please,' she says, yawning.

Rushing over, I pick up a book, pretend to consider

reading it then place it down on top of my phone. She doesn't seem to notice.

Her eyes are closed and her nose scrunches up as she wriggles further down in the bed, letting the covers touch her chin. 'It's cold in here.'

I climb into bed with her and place my head on the pillow next to hers. Up close, I can see the freckles on her nose, which she tries to hide with make-up before school. I don't know why, I always liked them.

'Alex?' I whisper, wondering if she's already asleep.

'Hmmm?' she murmurs.

'Do you remember that trip to Thurso with Mum and Dad?'

'The one where you broke the key in the lock at the B&B and we had to get the manager to fish out the broken pieces with a screwdriver?' she laughs, opening her eyes.

'Yeah,' I smile. 'Remember I was in charge of setting the alarm the next morning for the boat tour and I set it for 8.00 p.m. instead of 8.00 a.m.!'

She scrunches her nose and says, 'Dad was so angry. We all woke up after ten, and missed the boat! He'd already paid for our tickets up front and there was no refund. He refused to book again for the next day!'

'I'm sorry,' I say, brushing a strand of hair from her forehead. 'I know you really wanted to go on that boat ride. That was your choice, and I messed it up.'

'I didn't care about that stupid boat ride –'

'Yes you did –'

'No I didn't. I wanted to spend the day with you, and I did. I didn't care what we did on holiday. I just wanted to hang out with you. That was all I cared about.'

I smile and snuggle closer to her. I haven't lain in bed with my sister since we were kids. Being with her tonight makes me feel young again. Being with him doesn't. I feel tired, worn out, old.

'What's wrong?' she asks.

'Nothing,' I lie, hoping she doesn't see through it.

'It must be something. You haven't been yourself in a while. Are you and James fighting?' 'Sort of . . .'

She rolls over to face me. 'When?'

'Recently.'

'I knew something was wrong.'

I roll onto my back and stare up at the pale blue ceiling. I had painted it myself, back when all I had to think about was going to school with my friends and painting my nails a different shade each week. Everything had seemed so easy then, now it seems so trivial, like I had been fooling myself into thinking that this was living.

I had picked this particular shade of blue for the ceiling because it had reminded me of the sky on a clear sunny day, sitting on a blanket in the garden. And like tonight, it had reminded me of lying on the grass, staring up at the sky, while my sister lay next to me.

At first it looks perfect. But when I look again, tiny cracks spread through the paint like growing cobwebs, blemishing a seemingly flawless canvas. Perhaps like me. And perhaps like me, it wouldn't take much to bring it all down.

When did everything get so complicated? When did my decisions turn into my choices? I don't feel like I chose this for myself. I'm not happy. How could I choose something that doesn't make me happy?

And like she always does, my sister rests her hand on my arm, immediately making me feel like my old self, the one that once seemed so free and unburdened.

'You know, Liv, maybe it's not a bad thing if you break up. You've seemed so miserable the past few months. This might be exactly what you need right now.'

'Yeah, I know I've been so crabby. I'm sorry.'

'Why didn't you tell me?'

'I don't know. I should have.'

She frowns and looks at her chipped mint-green nails as she clutches the quilt edge tighter. 'We don't do this enough.'

'Sleep in the same bed?' I laugh.

'No, hang out just the two of us. We used to do it all the time.'

I gently touch her hand. It feels familiar, like my own hand. 'We still can.'

She snorts and rolls her eyes.

'What? I want to hang out with you, I do,' I say.

'You don't have to. You have your own life. You have your friends, and you'll sort everything out with James,

I'm sure. You only have six months left of school then you'll be off. You won't want to come back here.'

'Of course I will. I'll be coming back to visit you and Mum and Dad.'

'Once you leave, you won't look back,' she says quietly.

'Don't say that. I'll be back to visit all the time. And you can come to London to see me. We can go shopping and see a theatre show. It'll be so much fun . . . like Greece.'

At that moment, my phone beeps.

She smiles awkwardly, and rolls onto her other side. 'If it's James, you shouldn't answer that,' she mutters.

Clutching the phone to my chest, I sit up and slide my legs off the bed. Hunched over, the light from the screen straining my eyes slightly, I touch the message to open it.

I can't meet tomorrow – it's Hogmanay.

My fingers type frantically. Taking a deep breath, I re-read my reply:

It's tomorrow night or never.

My phone lights up again.

OK. I'll pick you up. Where will you be?

No. I don't want to tell him where I'll be. Tomorrow night is a chance for a new beginning, a new decision. I'll meet him, end this for ever, even if it means telling his wife, then I can go back to my friends, back to my old life, and ring in the new year with this great weight lifted off my shoulders. I need to do this before midnight. Midnight is mine. He won't take it from me.

So I respond:

No. I'll come to you. I'll pick you up at the bottom of your street at 10.30 p.m. and we'll go somewhere quiet where we can talk.

My wife will be suspicious if I suddenly leave. What am I supposed to tell her?

Lie. You're good at that.

Chapter Twenty-Six: 23.01.2016

Floorboards creak outside my door. A shadow appears under the edge, in the gap between the door and the carpet. Someone's standing there, waiting.

I don't get up to answer, I wait for them to knock. And when they do, I don't respond – I just want to be left alone today.

My dad is standing in the doorway to my bedroom. He's wearing his khaki green walking boots, thick parka coat and is holding his gloves in one hand.

'Are you going for a walk?' I ask.

'Yeah . . . do you want to come?'

I stare at him for a moment, not sure if I heard right. Walks were usually a time when he and Olivia talked about their week, whatever book they were reading, a TV show they enjoyed together. Occasionally they would stumble across a wildflower they didn't recognize and pick it to bring home to me. Usually I already had it, but every now and then, it was new to me. It was special.

They never talked about London. No, my dad didn't want to know about London, the place that was going to take his eldest daughter far away and tempt her to never come back.

But they liked their walks.

'I'd love to,' I finally say, getting up off the bed.

He waits for me downstairs as I change into warmer clothing.

And when I come down, he's holding my scarf and gloves in his hands. 'It's cold outside,' he says, handing them to me.

He holds my coat out, while I slide my arms in, and opens the door for me, gesturing me out first.

We drive down to Binscarth Woods, and park. The smells of the forest on a wet rainy day fill my nose and surround me.

Last time I was here, we were looking for Olivia. Last time I was here, I stood in a line with others, walking inch by inch, searching for her body. I remember feeling so confused, not knowing where she was or why she hadn't called home. I remember feeling so scared, and so alone.

I had been with my dad that day too, but today feels different. So much has happened since that day. It had been so loud, everyone calling her name. But now, it's so quiet. The only sounds are from the trees and the birds.

Trees don't fill the landscape of Orkney as they once did. They once covered the ground that we walk on. Honeysuckles. Junipers. Aspens. Willows. They were all here once. But like with everything, change comes.

And with change, often comes the end of one thing before another can begin.

But Orkney is fighting against this particular change. The council is trying to rebuild Orkney's forestry with their Woodland Project. Soon the island will look like Binscarth Woods.

And Olivia won't be around to see it.

Olivia won't be around to see a lot of things.

'I'm sorry, Alex,' says my dad eventually.

'You have nothing to be sorry about.'

The dead wintery shrubbery cracks and shatters under our boots as we walk. He doesn't look at me as he talks, but he looks out towards the path. 'You've been spending so much time with that detective –'

'Dad –'

'I didn't understand at first. Then I realised, you needed someone to talk to, an adult to . . . help you through this, help you understand what all this is. And that wasn't us. Your mother and I weren't there for you. We were grieving ourselves, but we should have been grieving as a family, and I'm so sorry.'

He stops and turns to me. As the sun rises, soft amber hues brush his cheeks. His brown almond-shaped eyes glimmer like Olivia's used to, when she was trying not to cry.

'You just reminded us so much of Olivia, and that's not fair on you. You shouldn't have had to cut your hair off to show you're not her. We shouldn't have –'

'I just thought I could help the detective inspector. I

just needed to feel like I was helping in some way, like I was useful.'

'You don't have to be useful. You're fifteen, you should be allowed to just be fifteen.'

'I'm sixteen, actually,' I mutter.

'Oh god,' he says, putting his hand to his face. I can see he's crying. 'I'm so sorry we missed your birthday.'

'It's OK. It's OK.'

He squats until he's low to the ground and eventually pulls his hand away from his face. Once he rises, he places a hand gently on my arm. 'How are you? Have we ever asked that?'

'Dad,' I stammer, as tears flow down my face. 'I'm just so tired. I don't know how much more I can take.'

He takes me and holds me close. His chest heaves in and out as he cries with me. 'I know, my darling. Me too.'

We stand in Olivia's forest, her safe haven, and we hold each other, each remembering a different part of her that we loved, that we miss. The breeze flows around us, empty winter branches bending and crackling.

And when we let go, everything still feels different, but better. I can finally see some light at the end of this long dark tunnel.

And I know I won't be alone in it any more.

I'll have my dad.

I'll have my mum.

And they'll have me.

When we return, Detective Inspector Birkens' car sits in the driveway. The door opens easily, pushed by the gentle wind. In the kitchen, Birkens stands against the counter, half-empty mug beside him. My mum sits at the dining table opposite him, cradling her mug of coffee like Birkens does.

'Is everything OK?' I ask, as we enter the room.

My mum nods quickly. 'The police have news.'

We sit beside her, all perched at the dining table, my dad and I still in our coats and gloves.

'We finally have forensics back on Olivia's laptop and I think we've got him.'

'You know who it is?' asks my dad, leaning in.

'Is it that other boy from S.A.D.? Nick something?'

'No, his alibi checks out, but we're close to finding out the identity. Forensics found a series of email exchanges with an address unknown to our investigation. We have a technology specialist in Glasgow that reviewed the files on the computer –'

'How?'

'We ran a forensic examination starting with a digital mirror image of the computer's hard drive. We then looked at Olivia's internet history, frequent search terms, and so on. What we did find were fragments of emails captured by the computer's memory from a repeated email address sent from a static IP address, which we linked to an address in Kirkwall.'

'Is that it? That's where the murderer lives?'

'No, that's the address of a café.'

'So what does that mean?'

'It means the person sending Olivia emails, sent some of them from this café. So, if we cross check the subscriber's dates – when he sent an email – with CCTV footage from the café, which we obtained this morning, we should get our guy.'

'How long will that take?'

'Not long. We have a team going through hours of CCTV footage so we should have a suspect within the next twenty-four to forty-eight hours. My suggestion to you is to stay put, and wait for my call.'

'That's it?'

'There is one more thing. The autopsy found traces of farm material, specifically a kind of hay or straw. We're conducting thorough checks on all farm properties within a certain radius of where the body was found. But like I said, twenty-four to forty-eight hours max. This will be over soon.'

'Thank you,' says my mum. 'I know we haven't said it since this started, but really, thank you.'

'We're going to get this guy.' He nods, slides his mug away, and slips out the front door.

As his car pulls out the driveway, the sound of the engine fading in the distance, we glance up at each other, finally seeing each other for the first time in weeks.

My mum rises first. She rushes me, throwing her arms tightly around me. My dad stands next, wrapping himself around us both.

It's almost over.

We made it.

We survived.

We can finally just grieve together, knowing the person who took her from us is locked up, in a dark place where he can't hurt anyone again.

After we stop crying, we do something I never imagined us doing again, or wanting to do again. We made dinner together, as a family.

We didn't say much, still reeling from Birkens' news.

And it's not the same. It's far from the same.

But it's a start.

Chapter Twenty-Seven:
24.01.2016

School drags on, each hour worse than the one before.

Classes, students, hallways. It's the same. It's always the same. No wonder Olivia was desperate to leave this place.

I don't talk to anyone in class any more, not even the teachers. I sit alone at lunch. Andy and Siobhan don't even try to talk to me now. I've lost everyone around me.

I'm empty inside. I feel nothing, and yet everything all at the same time. I'm sad, angry, anxious. There are reminders of Olivia everywhere. I pass her classrooms, I see James outside my window during Biology as he makes his way to Free Study, I even walk through the hallway by the girls' loo where she and Emily would meet to walk to lunch together.

She's everywhere here.

It's lunchtime. I'm not hungry so I decide to go outside for a jolt of cold air to my body. I need to feel something.

When I get to the double exit doors, I see Andy and Siobhan hugging in the courtyard outside that connects the chemistry wing and the library. I start to walk back inside, but my feet stop moving. I need to start repairing this friendship. I can't shut people out for ever.

I take a deep breath and push the doors open. A burst of wintery air hits me, and I immediately wake up. But as I get closer, I realize they aren't hugging. They're kissing. I don't know why it hurts, but it does. I have no reason to be angry, or do I? Andy and I were just starting something. Yes, I haven't talked to him in a few weeks but I've been sort of busy. He could have waited for me. But everyone's stopped waiting, everyone's stopped caring. Olivia's death is old news now. The killer's long gone according to the newspapers this morning. Portugal or France maybe. So everything is back to normal. No need to dwell on it any longer, right?

How dare they? How dare they move on without me? Cowards.

Did I mean nothing to Andy? Did our kiss mean nothing?

We can't go back to normal after this. This betrayal has split our group, and this can't be blamed on me. I may have been distant, even cold at times, but I just needed some time. I needed to grieve, to miss my sister. And where were they? Moving on apparently.

I'm angry, but it's not just about this. It's about everything. I hate everyone.

My hands are on Andy and Siobhan before I know

they are. She's screaming at me. He's yelling at me. People are staring. People are always staring.

'Stop staring!' I scream at a group that's gathered to see the drama unfold.

'Alex, what the hell?' yells Siobhan. She's on the ground. Why is she on the ground? Did I push her?

'What are you doing? How long have you been sneaking around?'

Olivia snuck around. She lied to me. She betrayed me.

'We just started going out. Why are you so upset?' Andy says to me.

I shake his arm off. Don't touch me. 'Because I thought *we* were going out!'

'We haven't talked to you in weeks.'

'Shut up, Siobhan. This is between me and Andy. I expected this from you, not him.'

'What is that supposed to mean?' she yells.

'You're always jealous of me! Always want what I have!'

'You're angry about your sister, I get it, but stop taking it out on us,' Andy says, trying to touch my arm again. I swing my hand out and it connects with Siobhan. She stumbles backwards, and stares at me for a long moment. Then she's back up and pushing me.

My body pushes into hers and we start grabbing at each other's clothes and hair. I don't know why this is happening. I don't want to hurt her. I don't want to hurt him. I'm not even sure if I'm that angry about this. I just know I feel anger burning through my body and I don't know how to stop it from taking over.

I feel hands on me, pulling me backwards away from her. A teacher. There's another one holding Siobhan back as she wildly swings her arms about telling people that I started it, that I'm crazy.

As I get dragged to the headmistress's office, I glance back and see Andy still in the courtyard. His expression of shock and confusion makes my cheeks burn. I feel so stupid, so immature. Fighting with my best friend over a boy. I'm not that person.

When we get to the office, Mrs Greene is sitting at her desk.

'Wait here,' says the teacher. I recognize her, but I don't think I've taken any classes with her, and I really hope I won't have to in the future.

She disappears into the office and leans into the headmistress. She nods her head and looks over her shoulder at me.

A few students are watching me from the office window. I guess they're looking for more drama.

'Why are we here, Alexandra?'

Mrs Greene is back behind her desk. The other teacher is gone and the door is closed.

Her office is small, a little cramped. Several photo frames adorn the white-washed walls, with some on shelves and on top of the filing cabinets by the door. Photos of student achievements, of field trips, concert performances. I'm sure if I looked, I'd see a photo of

Olivia dancing in a school concert somewhere. There would be no photos of me. I had achieved nothing, and maybe never would.

When I glance back, Mrs Greene is still staring at me. She wants a response, any response.

'I didn't start it,' I eventually say.

'Fighting? This isn't you.'

Maybe it is now. I'm just so angry all the time.

'I know. I'm sorry.'

'What happened?'

'It was a stupid argument that got out of hand. It was nothing really.'

'You needed two teachers to break it up. That's not nothing. That's serious. We don't tolerate fighting on school grounds. And Siobhan Mathers? You used to be best friends with her.'

'People change,' I shrug.

She leans forward and I know this is serious. Here we go, another lecture from an adult who knows nothing about what's going on inside my head. I didn't sign up for a counselling session. Just deal me the punishment so I can leave this office.

'Go on, get out of here,' she says gesturing towards the door.

'That's it?' I ask.

'I know what you and your family have been going through. I'm not going to call them with this. They have enough to deal with. Just no more fighting, OK, Alex?'

'Thank you.'

I lock my fingers together and head for the door. Maybe I'll just go home now. I've had enough of school, and it's probably had enough of me. I came back too early. I don't feel ready for this life yet.

Suddenly something on the filing cabinet catches my eye. It sits in a wooden frame, the corner of the wood chipped like it's been dropped. My sister's smiling face stares back at me. 'Mrs Greene, what is this photo?'

'It's the S.A.D. club – Schools Against Drugs. Your sister joined this school year. They really helped raise awareness about drug safety. You should have seen their council presentation back in October –'

'But . . .' I can't breathe. I can't focus. My eyes start to blur and the room begins to spin. What is happening? Am I really seeing this? 'This guy right here, beside Olivia . . .'

She walks over to me and takes the frame in her hands, and smiles. 'That's Officer Allans, well I guess it's Detective Constable now. He was the school resource officer for the Schools Against Drugs club. He handled a lot of the after-school meetings. Thursdays, I think. Why, do you know him?'

'Yes, I know him,' I mutter, my jaw tensing.

Everything becomes clear. It's like a fog lifting on a dark gloomy day, peeling back from the rooftops it clung to until all that remains is a bright blue sky. The room stops spinning, and my eyes target the frame. The way he stands beside her, the closeness of their shoulders, the way my sister slightly turns her body in to him. Even their smiles match, both hiding a secret she thought we'd never discover. A secret that hid a reality so far removed from her everyday life. It doesn't make sense, yet it does. This is why she was so secretive about him.

He's a police officer. A detective-in-training now.

And he's *married*.

She had so much to lose with this getting out. He had more to lose.

It's him.

Why didn't we know about this? Why didn't we see this?

I start running, my feet pounding the hallway. Mrs Greene is calling my name but I don't turn around. I can't. I have no time. My shoulders bump students, and I occasionally stumble as my eyes search frantically for the exit door. A group of students texting on their phones and gossiping break apart, and I see the door.

My hands push the silver bar and a gust of wind rushes in. The icy chill washes over me, but my body burns like it's on fire.

It's him.

My thighs throb but I don't stop running. I have to reach Birkens, I have to see him.

I can't believe this. How *could* she? My sister, my friend. This isn't her. She's not this person. How could *he*? I trusted him. My parents trusted him. Detective Inspector Birkens trusted him.

Seagulls swoop high above me and I know I'm

253

reaching the bay. The smell of salt is thick in the air. Engines churn and horns call from the deep bellies of the ferries that pass from Stromness to Graemsay and on to Moaness.

Seconds pass. Minutes close in. How long have I been running for? My feet slow to a walking pace as I desperately gasp for air. A pain forms in my left side, but I can't rest. Cars overtake me, giving me a wide berth.

The sun is setting in front of me. The reds blaze and the pink hues explode across the skyline. A couple of birds soar overhead, and remind me of the effortless way my sister danced. The pirouettes, the turns, the battements. She was so beautiful when she danced. She spread her arms out wide, like wings on a bird. Sometimes she closed her eyes and I wondered what she saw in the darkness.

Did she see me?

I always saw her.

The sun shimmers off the water, as I get closer to Birkens' cottage. The colours dance on the edge and graze the blue surface of the bay.

The pain deepens in my side and soon spreads to my belly, deep inside. I stop and lean over, and feel my face tense as the tears burn my eyes.

Is it him? Is this really going to be over?

I throw my head back to the sky and inhale a deep breath. It gets stuck in my throat. Coughing, I throw my hands down on the ground and catch myself.

Birkens' cottage is so close. *I'm* so close.

Keep going.

Keep going.

My legs start pushing forward again and my arms swing by my sides as I float in the air. My feet hit the soft ground and barely make a sound. A ferry emerges from behind a rock and drifts through the water, small waves hitting against the side of the hull.

The thatched roof of Birkens' cottage appears before me. The sunset flickers off his kitchen window, which faces the bay.

Please be home.

My body smashes into his door, and I knock frantically before turning the handle. It's unlocked, so I push through the door.

'Detective Inspector!'

I glance up the stairs, before heading into the kitchen. 'Detective, I know who it is! I know who killed Olivia. He's been right under our noses the entire time, I'm such an idiot! It's –'

My words catch in my throat, and I can barely breathe.

Standing in Birkens' kitchen is DC Allans.

His face tenses and I don't know what to do. Run? Fight?

He sees me hesitate and for a moment I think he's going to head towards me. He doesn't but in that moment, I hitch back and it's enough for him to startle. It all happens so fast. I'm there, standing there in Birkens' kitchen in front of the wooden shelving unit where he keeps the photo of his son. And the next second I'm on the tiled floor lying beside it.

My head throbs. Pain like I've never felt. And a warm sensation at my right temple. I touch the skin and when I pull my hand away, blood stays on my fingertips. Is that my blood?

Everything is hazy now. I'm tired. My eyelids are heavy. I don't want to sleep but my body fights my mind. I'm falling into darkness.

DC Allans is standing beside me with a flashlight in his hand. But he's holding it at the wrong end. The bulb is facing down and the handle is up. There's red on the handle. Blood. My blood.

It's him.

Darkness is near me, too close. It won't let me escape this one. I can't keep my eyes open.

I'm falling.

Chapter Twenty-Eight: 24.01.2016

I feel the gravel beneath my cheek first, then eventually the cold flooring beneath my limp body. I'm on my side, my arm is splayed out and when I go to move it, a dull ache passes over it. I've been in this position for a while now, because my neck is killing me.

My head throbs and when I touch it, a sharp pain explodes from my skull. I've been hit. Something – or someone – has hit me. My eyes are blurred, and I can barely see a metre in front of me. Am I blind? My hands feel around and I touch dirt, stones, and, somewhere underneath, cold wood. I'm inside, I must be. But where?

I curl my legs up and rock gently to the side until my knees are underneath me. My fingers reach up but don't connect with a ceiling so I must be able to stand up.

A noise from above startles me, and I immediately curl back into position. Footsteps scrape against wood and thump in a descending order – stairs. I must be underneath stairs of some kind, maybe in a cellar? The steps are getting louder, closer. Someone's coming.

A door opens somewhere near me, and I close my

eyes. I concentrate on relaxing my whole body so it looks limp again. My feet weigh down heavily on the floor, my side, my arm, everything is frozen and heavy. I slow my breathing down and deepen its sound. I want him to think I'm still unconscious. I need more time to come up with a plan.

The footsteps shuffle beside me until they're next to my head.

Please don't hurt me any more.

I feel hands on my arm, and I realize he's shaking me. But I stay limp, screaming only inside my head.

The hands are off me, and the footsteps are fading out. He's walking away. He's up the stairs, the thumping is getting softer. The door slams, but I wait. What if he's testing me?

Moments pass, seconds, maybe minutes.

My eyelids blink open and I shift my head up slightly. I don't see anyone here. It seems to be getting lighter, unless my eyes are adapting to the dark. I can now see my confinements.

My body lies in a small rectangular room. There are no windows, but light streams in from under the door. There's wooden shelving in the corner with some old paint tins at the bottom, and some bales of hay in another. It is a cellar. But the smell is different. It's sharp and familiar, but not a smell that I experience every day. It reminds me of the McGregor farm. It's a farm, or a stables of some kind because I smell horses everywhere.

Horse stables? Didn't Birkens say the police were looking at farms within a twenty-mile radius? They must see this on the map. They'll be coming soon, they'll find me. But DC Allans is the police. The police can't help me. He's one of them. And he's the killer.

What if no one comes for me?

I need a plan.

I can't stay here. If I stay, I die. Like Olivia.

I tuck my feet underneath me again and slowly rise up, one vertebrae at a time until I'm standing. The ceiling is low but doesn't touch me. The space is bigger than I first thought. Hay is scattered around, mixed in with dry soil and pebbles.

I need to find a way out.

My fingers lightly graze the walls as I search for the door. My thumb bumps something hard and cold, and metal. A door handle. I push down but it doesn't move. It's frozen, like I was on the floor. I push again. I'm locked in here.

There has to be another way out.

My hands search the walls again, this time more frantically. All I feel is cold rough brick and stone. There are no windows, no other doors, and no way out.

My finger grazes something sharp and I bite my lip to stop from screaming out. My finger stings, a sharp pain like my head. I touch it with my other hand and it's warm and sticky. Blood. I place my finger in my mouth and suck gently. Bitter and thick, the blood trickles down my throat into my belly.

I feel dizzy. I hate blood.

I sit down and feel my stomach churn. My head hurts more than ever. My vision is blurring again. No, not again. I'm going to pass out. I grip the wall and bite my lip, urging my body to fight the darkness again but I can't stop it. It's coming.

It's here.

When I wake again, the cold welcomes me. It's night. I know because it's pitch black and my body is shivering desperately in the cold.

I shuffle closer to the door, where light trickles under like water from a stream. There must be a lamp out there. I cling to it like a life jacket, hoping it will uncover something that can help me – a way out, a weapon, anything. My eyes search for movement under the door, but beyond nothing shifts. My hands try the door handle again, but it remains locked.

My head pounds, an endless headache with no moment of relief.

I'm thirsty.

I'm hungry.

What is he waiting for? For me to die in here like Olivia?

I curl my legs up and tuck my chin to my knees. My mum and dad's faces appear before me, like they're here with me. My dad has tears in his eyes – another daughter lost. Another death to grieve. In the darkness, in the corner farthest from the door where there should be shadows, my sister stands. She's wearing her mint-green jumper, the one that fastens at the shoulder. She's touching her favourite necklace, the one with the O, which she always fidgeted with. Mum would get so annoyed, telling her to leave it alone. But she couldn't help it. She loved to slide the O along the chain.

She's worried for me, I can tell. Her face is tense and she's looking towards the door.

Someone's coming.

I rush back to where I lay before and spread out on the floor again. A rustling of keys and a heavy strike against the door tells me there's a sliding bolt and likely a separate lock that needs a key.

Impossible to get out.

The door opens, and light streams in, touching every wall and corner. My sister's gone, as are my parents. It's just me in here. And him.

'I know you're awake. I heard you moving around.' He nudges my body with his boot, and I slowly open my eyes.

It is him. Detective Constable Dave Allans. Birkens' partner, and seemingly his friend. I gradually sit up and scoot my body back against the wall, as far from him as possible.

He seems different to me now. I don't know how I ever trusted him.

He crouches down to my level and stares at me. The soft expression on his face has been replaced by something much worse, more sinister. This isn't the man who took my statement the morning we reported Olivia missing, the same person who touched my shoulder and told me everything would be OK in the woods during the search party.

He knew we wouldn't find her, because he had her here at his farm, maybe even right here where I'm sitting.

'Why are you doing this?' I eventually ask, needing to fill the silent air between us.

'I'm so sorry. I never intended any of this to happen.'

'Liar,' I say, my jaw clenched.

'It's true. When I met Olivia that night, I just wanted to talk to her. But she was drunk, yelling at me. She was acting crazy –'

'No! She wasn't drunk. She was driving. She never would have drunk and got behind the wheel.'

'She was definitely upset though. And she was saying things, like she was going to tell my wife . . . I loved her, I never would have hurt her on purpose!'

'Then why is she dead?!' My shout hits off the wall and bounces back to me.

'We were arguing and I was holding her. I let go and she fell. I tried to wake her, I did. But I thought she was dead. If I knew she was alive I would have called an ambulance immediately. But I thought she was dead. She wasn't moving!'

But she was alive. My sister was alive. And now I'll never know what she was thinking right before she died. Did she think of me? Did she think of Mum and Dad? Oh god, was she scared?

'I was going to bury her somewhere – nicely of course. Put some flowers down. Then I was going to tip off the police so they'd find her and bury her properly so you and your parents could say goodbye. But when I came down that day, I found her in here – still alive. She'd been alive that entire time. So, I drove her to the Ring of Brodgar and left her there, hoping someone would find her. I didn't know she would die out there.'

He starts crying, softly at first, then deeper, more desperate. 'I didn't mean to kill her, I really didn't!'

I scoot forward a little closer, and try to soften the angry expression on my face.

I can do this.

'You didn't do anything wrong. It sounds like an accident to me, and it will to everyone else. I'll tell the police that. I'll tell them I fell and hit my head, and you took care of me. You helped me. Just let me go, and this will all go away –'

He stops crying and looks at me. 'I'm so sorry, Alexandra, but I can't do that. I can't afford to lose everything – my family, my job. I can't go to jail, I won't survive in there –'

'You won't go to jail –'

'I will. I know how this works. Even if her falling and hitting her head was an accident, I'll look guilty. Plus I didn't report it. I hid her body. They'll lock me up forever and throw away the key. I can't take that chance –'

'No, wait –!'

'I have to end this tonight. Then it will all go away. For ever. I'm sorry, but you need to die.'

Chapter Twenty-Nine: 24.01.2016

I remember the first time I saw Olivia dance.

It was the school Christmas concert. I sat in the audience between my mum and dad, waiting for the curtain to go up. It was the longest five minutes of my life.

Around me, friends laughed, families snuggled closer together. I waved to Siobhan, who was sitting with her mum and brother. Her dad worked offshore and was often gone for four or five weeks at a time. She didn't know if he'd be back for Christmas that year. I would later find out that he made it back in time to surprise them on Christmas Eve.

Mr Sheffield took to the piano that sat beside the stage, and started to play 'Hark the Herald Angels Sing'. Then the fifth-year choir began singing. And then, the curtain started ascending. Inch by inch it revealed a wide wooden stage festooned in white fairy lights and white fabric draped everywhere. It was beautiful. And at the centre was my sister.

She was wearing a long white chiffon dress, cut up to the thighs to show her silver dance leggings. She had on her new pointe shoes, and within moments she was twirling on her toes. The chiffon billowed out and floated in the air with her, as she spun around and around. Her hands stretched out high like she wanted to touch the night sky above. Under the stars, she danced. And I told myself she danced for me.

From that night on, I knew she was different from everyone around us. She was special. I blended into a crowd, a head in a sea of them. But she lit up the room. All eyes were on her. I loved her so much.

But that was also the night I experienced another emotion, something much deeper. For the first time in my life, and it wouldn't be the last, I felt envy. I was jealous of my sister, of her talent, of her ability to draw attention like a magnet.

I feel shame for thinking that now.

Because she would never be envious of me. She would be happy for me. And that just makes me more jealous of her. Deep down I always knew she was a better person than me.

I see her now.

She's standing over me, wearing that white chiffon dress, a crown of bluebells on her head. Her long hair flows over her shoulders and down her back. Her lips are red and rosy, her almond-shaped brown eyes are wide and open, and her hand is stretched out like she wants me to take it. But when I reach out, she drops it and shakes her head. She doesn't want me to go with her.

She wants me to fight.

My hands reach up again, but this time I place them

on DC Allans' wrists and I dig my nails in as hard as I can. He whimpers but doesn't take his hands off my neck.

I'm starting to lose consciousness now. I can feel the shadows creeping in, ready to take me. Darkness is waiting for me. But then I see white chiffon again.

Olivia.

I stretch my left hand out and touch something hard on the shelf beside my head. It's one of the paint tins. The thin metal handle slips through my fingers, and I prop my elbow on the floor to get some momentum. And I heave it towards him. It feels about half full, but it's heavy enough to strike him across the face and knock him off me.

When he rolls off, I jump to my feet and start running towards the light. My body crashes into the door and it swings open. I'm on the main stable floor now. Wooden cubicles line each side. At the far end is a double door on a latch. I keep running, until I reach the latch. It's broken and I slice my left palm on the metal fragments.

He's already here. He's rushing towards me. He's desperate to survive, as am I. I don't know who's going to be left standing at the end, but if it's not me I don't intend to make it easy for him.

I will fight him every moment until my last breath.

He charges me and I strike him with my arm, before we fall against the door. It opens up behind me, and I slide down it, scraping my head against the broken latch.

We're on the ground outside, stones and small pebbles

digging into my back. One hand is around my neck again, but this time my hands are cupped together and forced down by his other hand. I won't escape this one.

Olivia.

Help me.

I'm dying.

As the world around me fades, I feel an impact and gush of wind wash over my body. He's off me.

I think I see white fabric blowing in the breeze beside me but when my eyes clear, I only see Birkens' beige trench coat floating in the wind. He has Allans on his stomach on the ground and he's putting handcuffs on him. Officers stream past me and circle Birkens for support. Blue lights flash around me.

I'm safe.

Allans struggles against the officers and Birkens, and is roughly shoved into the back of a police van.

An officer helps me to my feet, and she's talking to me, asking me if I'm OK. Someone is putting a blanket over my shoulders, while another person directs a stretcher towards me. They tell me to sit down so they can look at my head injury but I push them aside. I start running, this time towards Birkens.

He turns and sees me, scooping me up into a deep hug. My blanket falls to the ground and my feet hover slightly.

I'm crying. He's telling me everything is OK, that I'm safe now.

I am.

I am safe.

He carries me to the stretcher and puts me down. Someone starts touching my face, prodding the cut on my temple. Then she begins wrapping my left hand, to stop the bleeding. It's deep. It might scar.

I grab Birkens' arm before he can leave. 'How did you know I was here?'

'We finally located the CCTV footage from the café where the IP address was picked up, and there he was. Allans. I couldn't believe it when I saw him, but it all made sense too, in a way. I checked into his background and found this property, left to him by his family. I had him meet me at my house, I had backup coming and everything, but you got there before I did. I never meant to put you in harm's way.'

I laugh shakily. 'Well, you did tell me to stop coming round, so I guess that's my fault.'

'And as usual you didn't listen,' he scoffs.

'I just can't believe it was him all this time.'

He shakes his head. 'Me neither. He was my partner. I should have known.'

'He had us all fooled, I guess. Even Olivia.'

He loosens his arms from my grip, and slides a hand into his pocket. He slowly pulls out a familiar thin gold chain.

'You found it!'

He drops the necklace into my right palm. 'One of my colleagues just found it downstairs in the cellar. I think where you were.'

'I knew Olivia had been there too. I just knew.' My fingertips gently play with the thin chain and trace the circular shape of the letter O. 'Will you put it on me?'

He smiles, and walks behind me. I lift my hair, and feel his fingers wrap the chain around my neck. He fiddles back there for a while, then steps back. 'Sorry, my hands are shaking.'

'Detective Inspector?'

'Yeah?'

'I want to go home now.' I slide down off the stretcher knowing I'll have to visit the hospital first. I might need stitches in my hand and head.

'Let's go see your mum and dad,' he says helping me to his car.

'You should too,' I say.

'What?'

'Go home. I think it's time.'

He opens the passenger side door for me, and looks up at the night sky, the stars dancing above us. 'Yeah, I think you might be right.'

Chapter Thirty: 31.12.2015

Olivia

I'm here. I left the party. And I left Emily. I didn't mean to keep anything from her. I just didn't want to tell anyone. *He* asked me not to tell anyone. But he also told me he and his wife were separated.

Everyone asked me where I was going and I lied. Like him, I am lying about where I am right now. But unlike him, I actually feel bad about it.

The way Emily looked at me when I told her I was glad to be moving to London and would forget all about her, is an expression that will haunt me for ever. How do you take something like that back?

I didn't mean it. Of course I didn't mean it. I was angry, and saying stupid things. She's my best friend and always will be. I want us to move to London together. We talked about it so much when we were kids. She danced too, until she fractured a bone in her ankle. Ever since then I can't help but feel like she's been jealous of me.

All she talks about now is working on her uncle's farm. She doesn't talk about London any more. But

I wanted her to come with me, to rent a small flat together, to explore the streets of London side by side.

She's changed, not me.

Or maybe I have, like she said back at the party. Maybe I'm different.

I don't know. I'm eighteen – my life is meant to be simple.

As the mist softens, the small houses appear, each tightly packed against the next one. How can people live like this?

I need space. I always have.

It had taken no more than fifteen minutes to reach his street. He lives close, too close. Everyone does, here. Our island is small. Too small.

It's pouring with rain. I can barely see three metres in front of me, but I immediately see him walking down the street, coming towards my car. I tense up and feel the butterflies in my belly getting stronger. I feel sick. I can't be here. I can't do this. Who am I kidding, I'm not ready to end this. I can't end this. He won't let me. This will keep going on and on until I crack, or until I move away. Perhaps I can keep this up until I leave for London. I can keep up the falsities and play along for another six months and then when I leave for London I'll finally be free of him and of this relationship. I won't have to go through this tonight. I won't have to look him in the eye and tell him that it's over and that he needs to stay away from me or else.

I lean forward and quickly turn the key in the

ignition, but before I can put my foot on the clutch, he's knocking on my window, telling me to unlock the door. I don't have to do it. I can stay here inside the car, safe. Why am I so scared of him?

This is ridiculous. I'm eighteen years old. I'm not a child and I can handle this. I lean forward and unlock the passenger side, letting him in.

He slides into the seat, shaking the rain off his coat sleeve and runs his hand through his damp hair. He turns to me and leans in. I move back.

'What's wrong?'

'I don't want to talk here. Is there somewhere we can go where no one will see us?'

'Drive up to the stables.'

I turn away from him, feeling his eyes still on me.

We drive past the beach, each turn feeling like another obstacle in my path. The sandy dunes rise up from the ground, and I take a left. I drive past the public parking sign and past the loading bay, where in only a few hours fishermen will gather to greet the trawlers and boats coming in. Once the fish and seafood is cleaned and inventories are taken, they're divided up into ice-packed boxes and loaded back onto boats to set sail for the mainland. Everyone wants food from Orkney but no wants to live here.

The bushes around us get thick as I drive away from the beach, further into the heart of the island. When I see the thatched rooftop of the old riding stables, I settle into a low gear and slowly pull up. Sliding the clutch into gear, I roll to a stop and pull up the handbrake. The sky is so clear here, even through the rain I can see the stars. Gone is the mist, and now everything is so clear.

I feel his hand in my hair, the strands curling around his fingers and I recoil.

'What's wrong, Liv?'

I can't breathe. It's so suffocating in this car, I need to leave. I need to get out.

I pull the handle towards me and my door pops open. Swinging my legs out, I step into the light rain.

'What are you doing?' he calls after me.

'It's too hot in there. I need some air,' I say, walking further from the car. I keep going until the trees are at my back and the stables sit in front of me.

I don't remember this place ever being open. It's so rundown now, I can't imagine people coming here to ride horses around the property. I wonder why they left all this to him? What has he done with it? Nothing. He left it to waste away until there was nothing left but a hollow shell.

What if he's done that to me?

He's in front of me now, blocking the stables. 'What is all this? Are you feeling OK?'

'I'm fine. I've actually never been better –'

'Good, I –'

'I can't do this any more.'

The air is thick and hangs between us.

'What?' he eventually says.

'The lying, the sneaking around. I can't do it any more.'

He reaches for my hand but I pull back. 'Look, I told you it's just for a little longer then –'

'Then what? Nothing! I'm sick of your empty promises! I'm sick of you stringing me along!'

'Calm down,' he warns me. He's getting tired of my feelings, I think. I'm too emotional for him, too attached. Sorry. I'll try to be clearer for him.

'I don't want you calling me, or texting me, or showing up at my school. I want you to stay away from me.'

'You're being ridiculous now, we live on the same island!' He's shouting. He's getting angry. He has no right to be angry with me.

'Don't call me ridiculous! I'm not being overdramatic!'

'No, you're just behaving like a child.'

'Of course I am, because I am one. I'm eighteen years old! How would your wife feel if she found out? Yeah, that's right. I know all about her!'

He steps forward, into my space. 'Don't you dare say anything about her, she has nothing to do with this.'

'Yes, clearly!'

'Stop being stupid, and get in the car.' He grabs my wrist and starts to drag me back to the car.

I'm not going anywhere with him. He can walk back to his house for all I care. It would only take him a half hour or so anyway. But I hope he gets drenched in the rain.

'Don't tell me what to do, and don't touch me.' I jerk my arm back, but he grips more tightly. He pulls me closer, so I'm practically nose to nose with him. His forehead is tense and his jawline pushes out.

'Let go!'

'Fine!' He lets go, but I'm not ready. My body weight is still tipping forward so I arch my back for support but feel myself falling the other way. I slam back onto something hard. I feel it in my head first. It explodes with pain then I feel warmth at the back of my head. My fingers reach behind, but my hand is trembling. When I pull my hand back, there's blood. So much blood.

I'm confused. Where am I? What happened?

Where did all this blood come from?

I open my mouth to say something, but the words are jumbled up. I'm stuttering, stuck on the first word. I don't even recognize my own voice. Who is this person trying to talk?

I'm so tired. I want to close my eyes and sleep for a little bit. I know deep down that's a bad idea, but I can't help it. My eyelids are so heavy.

I hear someone calling my name.

'Olivia!'

'Olivia!'

Who is this?

I can't see him properly. Everything is blurred. Splotchy, dotted, disfigured messages that I can't decipher.

I feel someone shaking my shoulders. I can't stop

staring at the night sky. I don't see much, but I see lots of little bright lights. Are they stars?

I must be outside because I'm cold, so cold. But my head feels warm, so warm.

I'm scared now.

My eyes are watering and spilling. I want to go home. I want to see my mum, my dad, my little sister.

Alex.

She'll be wondering where I am.

Where am I?

The little bright lights are moving now. They're sliding up the sky to the top. No, maybe *I'm* moving. I think I'm being dragged.

Alex.

Are you here?

I think I'm at the beach. Because it's bright and sunny, and the waves are lapping behind me. I see my sister. She's laughing. She wants me to chase her. She's so young, only about seven years old. I start chasing her. My feet land on the soft sand as I run. My hands are out to reach her, but I can never catch her. She's so fast.

The sun is setting behind her. Swirls and swishes of pinks and lavender look like they've been painted on with a brush. Beyond that, a clean canvas, ready to be made into something magnificent.

I'm tired, so I collapse on the warm sand and gently lie my head back until it touches the ground.

But now it doesn't feel warm, or sandy. The ground beneath my head is cold and hard. I'm not at the beach.

I'm still here, wherever that is. I'm still outside. No, now I'm inside, I think. But I'm still cold.

And I'm still scared.

Where did my sister go?

It's dark in here.

There are footsteps around me, shifting between my arms and legs.

Help me.

I try to say the words but I can't open my mouth fully. Instead a sound comes out. There are no words. Just sounds.

Help me.

The footsteps are getting quieter now. I think someone's leaving. They're leaving me here.

Please don't leave me.

I don't like the dark.

My eyelids are dropping now. I'm going to sleep a little. I'll feel better when I wake up. Just a quick nap. A few moments, that's all . . .

Alex, come find me.

Chapter Thirty-One: 28.01.2016

I wake early that morning, long before the sun has risen. I dress warmly, slipping into my thickest jumper and longest scarf. I leave before my parents have stirred, and head down the path towards the bus stop. Darkness is all around me, occasional lights from street lamps or cottage windows illuminating the walkway.

I wait only ten minutes for the bus and when I board, I'm the only one on it. The driver nods at me, recognizing me from the papers. He looks at the rear mirror and waits for me to sit before he starts the engine again. The road is bumpy, the corners sudden, the hills steep, but it's a path familiar to me now.

When we reach the B9055, the tips of the Standing Stones of Stenness materialize up ahead.

I'm almost there.

I step off the bus onto the early morning grass, slick with dew. The droplets slide against my boots as I walk towards the Ring of Brodgar.

When I reach the base of the hill, a metal barrier outlines a path up to the stones, ditches dense with heather on either side. The barrier meets at the top, looping around the circular stones, aimed at keeping out tourists until the sun rises. But I'm not a tourist. This place is in my blood, and always will be. I climb over the barrier and jump onto the dirt, walking on.

The breeze flows through my hair, pushing the strands out away from my hat. My fingers touch the scarf material, the soft fabric coiled around my neck, warm against my skin. My strides are wide, the soles of my boots slightly sinking into the frosty mud. By the time I reach the stones, the first glimmer of a new day is upon me, low in the sky. Streaks of coral and orange spread onto the grass and snake towards me.

Many of the stones are taller than I remember, some reduced to merely stumps rising from the ground. The history is palpable here, protected within the core of the stones. A large circle of heather sits and waits for spring to awaken its roots, murky soil threatening to bury it.

Clusters of daisies gather at the base of many of the standing stones, their petals white as the snow that blankets the earth beneath me.

Olivia loved daisies. She would make chains from their stems, and rest a daisy crown on her head as she sat outside in the garden, plucking blades of grass from the ground beneath her bare feet.

I remember the string of daisies that I laid around her head, just moments before her body was lowered into the ground.

It made sense that I visit today, just as it made sense

that my sister was left here. If she was to be taken from me, then I would want her final moments to be here among the stones. Long ago, people gathered here to pray for their Norse god, Wōden. He watched over Valhalla, welcoming those who had died in battle. Did he wait for her?

He was also known as Odin the Wanderer. That was my sister. She was a wanderer, always looking out the window, always beyond the confines of this island. But she knew where she was heading. She wandered, but was not lost.

I see the one that held my sister, protecting her until she was found. I would recognize it always.

I wrote a letter to the council yesterday, asking them for a small plaque in memory of Olivia. I don't know if they'll agree, it's a national heritage site; but I think they will read my letter and understand why my family and I want it.

I walk closer and reach my arm out. Wriggling out of a glove, I place my left palm flat against the cold stone, patches of yellow moss digging into my skin as I push hard. Hot tears prick my eyes.

My left hand is healing now, as is my head, but the skin will always carry the scars from that night. I pull my hand back and touch the bandage with my other hand. It still hurts, still feels raw. But I don't mind. Because it will heal. And although it will scar, possibly deep, it will always remind me of my strength and how hard I fought for my sister.

My sister was unbelievable to me. Infinitely extraordinary. Strong, brave, ambitious. A beautiful dancer. But most of all, she was my sister. Her presence in this world will haunt me, and those who really knew her. I will miss her every second of every day of my life, but I will remember that, unlike billions of people, I had the privilege of knowing her. I don't know what I'll do with my life after school ends, whether I'll stay on Orkney or leave to start a new life elsewhere. But I know she will always be with me. I touch the gold-plated O necklace around my neck and look out past the stones that circle around me like the letter in her name. It's almost time.

I start walking again, leaving the stones behind me to get smaller and smaller. The wind picks up the closer I get to the loch. The streaks of corals and oranges are deeper now, and stretching across the island. Some small fishing boats sit peacefully on the surface, barely breaking the water. The early morning glistens off the water, its reflection momentarily dazzling my eyes. I turn away for a second, then turn back to watch the ember glows build and flower into the sky, the petals blossoming wide.

By the time I reach the ferry terminal, the sky is bright once again, all traces of night burned away. I check my watch. He should be here by now, his ferry leaves in twenty minutes.

When I look up again, I see him standing there, clutching an oversized duffel bag in one hand, and a briefcase in the other. He sees me, because he's surprised but walking towards me. We meet at the ferry loading pier. There's barely twelve inches between us.

'What are you doing here?' he asks.

'I called the station, they said you were leaving on the 9.15 a.m. ferry.'

He lowers his head. 'I'm sorry I didn't tell you. I didn't want you to have to say goodbye. Not again, not after having to say goodbye to your sister.'

I nod, and look down at my shoes. Please don't cry. Please don't cry.

'Are you going home?' I finally say.

He smiles. 'Yeah. I am.' He looks out onto the loch, and nods his head. 'I'm finally ready to go home.'

'I'm so happy to hear that.'

'So was my wife,' he laughs awkwardly.

'It will be quiet around here without you.'

'Yeah, you'll have to find somewhere else to let your coffee get cold.'

I laugh, and immediately feel my face contort into a cry, so I tuck my chin to my chest.

'You'll be fine, Alex. You're strong. Like your sister.'

Kicking at the ground with my boots, I eventually glance back up to meet his eyes.

'I wish you could have known her. She would have liked you.'

'If she was anything like you, I think we would have got on just fine.'

Behind him the barrier lifts, and passengers slowly stream onto the ferry. He bends down and leans in, wrapping his arms around me. I bite my lip to stop the tears and nuzzle into his shoulder. When he eventually pulls away, he has tears in his eyes. Sliding his hand into his coat pocket, he pulls out the Superman keyring and uncoils a silver key, discarding it into his jeans pocket. He touches the keyring gently, small creases forming around his eyes. He takes my hand delicately and places the keyring into my palm.

'Take care of yourself, and your mum and dad.'

'Yeah, you too.'

Picking up his bags, he turns and starts walking towards the barrier.

'Detective Inspector?' I call after him.

'It's Daniel,' he says.

'Daniel?'

'Yeah?'

'Thank you,' I say, wiping away a tear with the back of my hand.

'No, Alex, it's me that should be thanking you. I'm getting on this ferry because of you.' He smiles and disappears beyond the barrier, it lowering behind him. No turning back now. His feet step onto the ferry and he immediately turns around.

I walk towards him until the barrier presses against my belly and I can't go any further. I watch as the ferry pulls out slowly. It turns towards the sunrise, and moves further and further away from this island, so he can finally say goodbye to his ghosts.

When all that's left is a dot on the water, I start

walking back home. The cool breeze hits my face and I take a deep breath in, feeling it wash over me. The Superman keyring dangles from my hand. I clutch it tighter, and tip my head back. Helicopters float high above me, their blades dark and sleek, like blackbirds soaring in the sky.

Author Acknowledgements

First and foremost I'd like to thank my family for their guidance and encouragement during this writing process, and during what turned out to be a challenging and emotional year for me. The loving support of my parents put me on the path to writing, and I will always appreciate their wisdom, praise and honesty. I have always looked up to my older brother, and he continues to be that role model for me. My sister is my biggest fan, and has been there for me through everything. I look forward to spending more time with my family this year.

Another nod to a fabulous and supportive team is to everyone at Peters, Fraser & Dunlop and HQ/HarperCollins for their efforts with *Dear Charlie* and *Blackbird*. In particular, Silvia Molteni who took an early chance with me and I will always be grateful for that; Anna Baggaley - thank you for your patience, guidance and encouragement.

I'll never forget my first writing class which helped me pick up a pen and paper (and eventually a laptop!) and do something that I'd always wanted to do but never thought I could – *write*. Thank you to my writing professor, T.M. Murphy, who read some very early work and encouraged me to move forward.

And lastly, I'd like to thank the people of Orkney, who welcomed me onto their island one windy and cold weekend as part of a research trip. The beautiful landscape of this place helped shape *Blackbird*.

HQ Young Adult
One Place. Many Stories

The home of fun, contemporary
and meaningful Young Adult fiction.

Follow us online

 @HQYoungAdult

 @HQYoungAdult

 HQYoungAdult

 HQMusic